SECRETS OF THE STRONGBOX

BILL ANDERSON

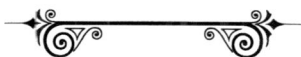

This book is dedicated to my wife, Deborah.

Her support and influence throughout this process has made

the publishing of these books

possible.

TABLE OF CONTENTS

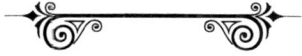

INTRODUCTION

Andrew Moss was the pen name I used when I wrote my first book, *The New Kid*. The book was about my 11-year tenure at the Woodstock Children's Home. That book, although names were changed, was an autobiographical memoir based on true stories and events that happened at the home while I was there and how they affected my life.

My nickname was "Andy." I am writing this book in the first person and I am the reporter in the story.

This book is fictional. Some of the "crimes," however, are based on incidents that happened there–most of the stories are amusing, but a few deal with some more serious issues. The events in the book take place in the time period of 1956–1967. None of today's technology is used. Watchers of *CSI* and *Law and Order* hopefully will not be disappointed. No cell phones, DNA matching or use of national crime data bases. I just report what I observed. I was once in a while involved in some of these capers, some I just heard about, some are based loosely on situations involving the kids at the home.

Author note: Throughout the book I add commentary based upon observations I have made throughout my life. I also attempt to include as much about Woodstock and local people and businesses as possible. While there are a lot of facts in the book, it is still a work of fiction.

Chapter 1

"MY BEAT"

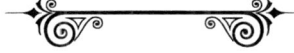

My name is Andy Moss. I am 13 years old. I have taken it upon myself to be the reporter of crimes committed at the children's home where I am a resident. I am not a "squealer." Squealers are abhorred at the home. After all, us kids are all in this together. Us against them. The kids vs. the house parents. We have to keep a united front against those who want to punish us and take away our privileges for petty crimes, mischief, mistakes we make and the general mayhem we sometimes cause.

My dream is to one day become the Crime Beat Reporter for our local newspaper, the *Woodstock Daily Sentinel,* where I worked as a paper boy for two years in the fourth and fifth grades. The *Sentinel* is just a small town paper now, but someday it could become part of a bigger news organization and I could become a household name. I hope to occupy one of those offices at the front of the building on Jefferson Street, just off the town square—sit there with my sleeves rolled up, tie undone and have an ash tray full of cigarette butts. I will probably never be famous, but I will do my best. My experience as the crime reporter for the home will provide valuable experience in preparation for my career ahead and will give me a leg up on the competition.

I don't have a phone booth like Clark Kent or a nice office like an adult reporter, but I do have my own "space." It is a little crude with no real amenities, but it is private. There is a small cottage located on the children's home property, just off the back porch of the main building. The cottage is a place for house parents to live. A tiny cottage with a basement underneath that contains the boiler room for the home and a small room with a work bench. The maintenance man for the home uses this area to keep tools needed for his work. The old boiler is huge and kind of scary. It is noisy and hot. You can hear it hiss and thump when you are in the cottage. The room is sooty and dark. No one really likes to go down there. That is why I have chosen that spot to be the location of my most prized possession.

I have a strongbox that holds my important materials. Pencils, spiral notebook, binoculars, magnifying glass, screwdriver set (who knows, I may need to pick a lock) and my Polaroid camera that develops pictures on the spot. My grandma Bolden gave me the camera for my 12th birthday.

We kids at the home do not have a lot of personal possessions and those we have need to be protected. We all have a foot locker at the end of our beds, but they are not locked. I always wanted a place where I could keep my things. It seemed that everything I owned could so easily be seen and observed by everyone else. There was just no privacy. I was unable to find anything suitable to use, until one day I just got lucky.

I was walking home from school one day and Mr. Dillon, at the corner of Grove and Seminary, was putting out his garbage. I knew Mr. Dillon from my paper route. He was a nice man, always gave me a dime tip each week and a dollar at Christmas. He once gave me a book entitled *Big Brother.* I remember enjoying the book. It was about a boy and a bear I stopped to visit with Mr. Dillon.

He was carrying this wooden box out to the curb. He was apparently going to put it out for the garbage men to take. He set the box down. I looked it over. The box was kind of mysterious–looked like it might have been used on a pirate ship. It was well put together, but the wood was rough. It was about two feet long, 18 inches wide and 18 inches deep. It had a top that would open and lay back on its hinges. The hinges on the box were brass and seemed rather large for the box. The box must have been used to store some pretty heavy items. Maybe gold coins or precious jewels. There was a hasp on the front of the box. It was brass also and had a large loop where a padlock would fit. The padlock must have been big and strong as well to provide for protection of whatever precious cargo was stored in the box. There were marks on the box. One mark looked like it might have been made by a sword or a very large knife. There were some reddish, black stains that looked like they may have been blood. I hope they didn't use the box as a place to behead enemies. There were some burn marks. The box had obviously been moved around a lot, despite its size, because the bottom was worn to an almost smooth finish.

Mr. Dillon noticed me admiring the box. He said, "Andy, you might like to have this box. It was my son's and he hasn't used it in years. I don't even remember where we got this box. It just seemed to be here one day." I remember his son Bob. Bob was several years older than me and was off to college.

I told Mr. Dillon that I definitely liked the box. I shared with him that I wanted a place to keep my own things. And that box looked liked it could protect anything! I told him that I would need to find a lock and key for it. He tilted back his cap, scratched his head and said, "You know, Andy, I just might have what you need." He went into his garage, shuffled through some items on his workbench and came back with a rather large lock. It wasn't brass and it looked a bit rusty, but there was a key attached to it. He said, "I think a little *3-in-1 oil* and a little elbow grease, we can have this lock looking like new."

We went to work on it. Used some steel wool, the oil and a wire brush. We worked on the box for about a half hour. He was right. It didn't take long. The lock looked a lot better and the key worked just fine.

Wow, I couldn't believe my good fortune. I now had my own box, with a lock and key, to protect my valuables! And not just any box, but a box that had probably come from a pirate ship! The box was heavy, but I was able to carry it across the street to the Harrison House, where I resided. Maybe someday I would be able to have a brass plate made that would have my name on it or maybe have someone carve my name into the wood.

15

There was a small broom closet in the basement of the cottage located behind the big scary boiler. It had a door and was filled with brooms, rakes and shovels. There was a shelf located about a foot off the floor with some paint cans on it and some rags. I was able to hoist the box onto the shelf and hide it under the pile of rags. Surely, no other kids would have any interest in going in that closet. I suppose the maintenance man might find it, but if he did, so what? It was locked and I had the key. There was nothing illegal in it. He would simply discover my crime reporting activities. Now I had my secret hiding place. I would go there many times over the years to make notes, retrieve my camera and add crime souvenirs. I never did pick any locks though.

Chapter 2

JAY'S HOBBY

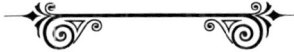

J ay had just finished collecting on his paper route. It was Saturday morning about 11:00. He usually collected the .30 per week for the *Daily Sentinel* on Friday nights, but there were always some people who were not home, so he would go out on Saturday mornings, which was fine. It gave him an excuse to get away from the home and the mundane chores that were required if you didn't have a job away from the home.

The kids at the home were supposed to turn in all money they received, from whatever source, immediately. The money was put into one's personal account for future use. Actually, two accounts were set up. One was a "spending" account to be used for personal items, such as clothing and things each kid might want, like a toy or a game. The other account was a "forced savings" account, to be used for college or maybe purchase a car when they left the home.

Jay was not good about turning in his money from the paper route. The house parents were always questioning him about how much money he made on his route. They knew he did a good job and made good tips. He would many times stop somewhere on the way home and spend some of the money. One of his favorite places was *Polizzi's* grocery store, located at "Six-corners," the intersection of Routes 47 & 120, North Street, McHenry and Seminary Avenues. Unfortunately, or maybe fortunately, depending upon who was looking at the situation, *Polizzi's* was one of the first stops on Jay's route and he would usually load up on pop and candy. Caz and Nick Polizzi were always nice. Jay also had to walk by *Strain's Pantry*. Jim Strain not only had a good selection of candy, but also sold comic books and baseball cards. There was just too much temptation at those two stores.

Today, after settling up his account at the Daily Sentinel, he had netted almost $8.00. The paper cost customers .30 per week. Jay got to keep .07 for each customer. Jay generally received about $5.00 per weeks in tips. He decided to go to the F. W. Woolworth store on the square. Jay had recently started collecting stamps and the store had a rack of them displayed over near the area of the store where fabrics were sold. The packets cost .10 each. Jay thought he could purchase a nice selection today.

The selection was awesome. Stamps from Germany, Sweden, Liberia, Cuba and even popular commemorative stamps from the United States. Jay had recently bought an album, "The Ambassador," a beginner's album, and he was anxious to fill it. Someday he hoped to buy the "Citation" album he saw in the H.E. Harris catalog that came in the mail. He reviewed the selections and decided which ones he would buy. He decided that the home would not realize that he had spent $1.00 of his earnings.

But there were two more packets that he really wanted–one a packet of three from the Pitcairn Islands and a packet of two U.S. airmails. The ones from the Pitcairn Islands were so pretty. They had the Queen of England's picture on them, as did almost all stamps from countries of the British Empire. The U. S. airmails were not real special, but he needed them to complete a page in the "Airmails" section of his album. He didn't want to press his luck with the home and get in trouble again because of spending his money before he got home. He was in a quandary.

He had never stolen anything before, but he really wanted these stamps, and he wanted them today. Maybe he could just "take" them today and then come back next week and tell the lady at the cash register that he had forgotten to pay for them and give her the twenty cents. That sounded like a good plan to him. He slipped those two packets in the right back pocket of his jeans. Surely, no one at the store would be suspicious of him since he was making a purchase. And the people in the store knew him. Why would they be suspicious today?

Unbeknownst to Jay, on the other side of the aisle was a door with a sign that read, "Employees Only." The door had a small glass window at adult eye level. The store manager, Mr. Hutson, was standing on the other side of the door and watched Jay slip the two packets of stamps in his pocket. As Jay was walking away from the display, he heard the door open and a man's stern voice say, "Hey, young man." Jay froze in his tracks.

Mr. Hutson took Jay by the arm and ushered him into his office located at the back of the store, behind a locked door. There was also a lady in the office running an adding machine, the kind with a handle that had to be manually pulled down after each entry. Mr. Hutson sat at his desk and told Jay to sit in the chair in front of it. The store manager went on to

20

explain to Jay that he could, and should, walk him across the square to the police station. The police were scary enough, but that old, abandoned opera house where the police station was located was spooky too. He asked Jay his name and also asked his parents' names. Jay explained that he didn't have parents, that he lived at the Children's Home. Mr. Hutson asked Jay what he thought the people at the home would do if they found out he had been caught stealing.

Jay looked down dejectedly and said he would probably "get the belt." "And be grounded," he added. Jay didn't tell Mr. Hutson, but he also thought that a lot more accountability would be required about his funds and his whereabouts. This bothered Jay even more. His paper route allowed him extra freedom and he would hate to lose that.

Mr. Hutson told Jay that if he had learned his lesson and would promise to never steal anything again in his life, that Mr. Hutson would not take him to the police and would not call the home. Jay hoped that he could trust the store manager. Jay considered this offer, and nodded his head in agreement. Mr. Hutson told Jay that this was a very serious matter. Jay was taken to one of the cash registers located at the front of the store and was required to pay for all 12 packets of stamps. Jay was told that he would be allowed back in the store, but should know that he would be watched by all store employees. Jay felt remorse, was ashamed and was still scared that somehow the home would find out. Luckily, they never did.

It was a long walk home from the square that day. Jay felt bad. He was so embarrassed. He wasn't sure he could face people at the store again. Kids from high school worked there. He hoped they wouldn't tell other kids about what he had done. And there was that older lady that knew Mr. Barry from the church. He hoped she wouldn't tell Mr. Barry. Jay had never stolen anything before. What a stupid thing to do! He vowed to himself that he would never steal again.

I had a stamp collection also. Jay and I would sometimes sit together at a table in the recreation room and work on our stamps together. It was while Jay and I were working on our collections one day that he told me this story. He had a hard time telling it, as he was still ashamed. Jay gave me a packet of stamps from the Pitcairn Islands and said, "You can have these, they are duplicates anyway."

I don't know if that packet was one of the two he had stolen or if they were actually duplicates. I put the stamps in my album, but I put the packet in my strongbox. Each time I see the packet, I am reminded that stealing is not a good idea.

Chapter 3

WARDROBE CHALLENGE

New clothes at the home were a luxury. Most came from one of two sources–gifts at Christmas, or "donations" as we called them. The Salvation Army would occasionally drop off a load of clothing at the home, and once a month kids from Wheaton College would bring clothing that had been donated by students and faculty there. Of course these weren't new clothes, but were usually better than what we had. They felt like new clothes to us. The clothing from the Wheaton College students was usually more fashionable as well.

Some of the teenage girls at the home, however, had developed a system of their own for obtaining new clothes.

There was a *Montgomery Ward* store located on the Woodstock square. It was a 3-story building located next to the local post office. The store was the retail anchor for the town.

One could buy nearly anything needed for the home from "Wards". It closed in 1972 and moved to Crystal Lake, where it had a much larger store with ample parking. On the rare occasion when we got to shop at "Wards", we felt as though we were shopping at *Marshall Fields or Bloomingdales*. I remember buying shoes there from Mr. Okey. He had children that went to school with us–Jim, Bonnie and Mary. Dick Mann got his start in the men's clothing business by working at the store.

We were required to walk to high school (unless the temperature was below zero degrees or raining very hard), which was more than a mile away from the home. The most direct route was to walk through the town square, where "Wards" was located. It was always fun to walk home through the square. We would sometimes stop at *"Hubert's Drug Store"* for a cherry coke or a green river. Jim Lippold worked there. The *News Depot* was a good spot too. They always seemed to hire cute girls, like Carrie Biel and Kris Luallen. It was always fun to stop and "sign up" at *Stone's*.

Beverly, Sandy and Linda were tired of dressing in less than stylish clothes at school. Back in the 1950's girls were still required to wear skirts and dresses to school. They would often stop at the Wards store on the way home from school to browse through the latest retail offerings. Sometimes they would try things on. This became a habit. They learned that it was easy to wear some larger clothing to school and then on the way home stop at Wards and put new clothing under it. They got pretty adept at this and even told some of the other teenage girls at the home what they were doing. The system was working pretty well for a time.

Mrs. Beard, the housemother at the time, began noticing that some of the girls were dressing more fashionably. One afternoon when the girls came home from school, Mrs. Beard said she would like to visit with them in the office. She said, "I have noticed that the three of you seem to have some new clothes. I don't recall taking you shopping. Can you tell me where the new clothes are coming from?"

Bev spoke up first. "One of my friends from school gave me the clothes. She had lost weight and they didn't fit her any longer." Mrs. Beard asked the name of the friend. Bev kind of stammered and offered up the name Elizabeth Boyles. Mrs. Beard wrote it down.

Mrs. Beard then turned to Sandy. "And how about you, Sandy?" Sandy had a babysitting and cleaning job at the home of a local businessman. Sandy said, "His wife bought me some new clothes because she felt sorry for me. Mrs.

Beard said, "I will have to talk to Mrs. Leucht" and wrote that information down.

Mrs. Beard looked at Linda. Linda said, "The last time my parents were here they gave me some extra money and said that I should buy some new clothes."

Mrs. Beard shook her head and told Linda, "Well, you know that you should have turned that money in to me to put in your account. We will deal with that issue later." She made another note on the paper in front of her.

Mrs. Beard then said, "Do you girls want to be present when I call these people to confirm your stories?" The girls looked at each other warily. They slouched in their chairs.

Bev said, "Can we just talk by ourselves for a bit?" The housemother just nodded her head, left the office and closed the door.

Bev turned to Linda and Sandy and asked, "Now what the heck are we going to do? I don't want her calling Elizabeth's mom."

Sandy remarked, "And I don't want to get Mrs. Leucht involved, even though she would probably cover for me."

Linda said, "My parents would be really teed off if they knew I was lying."

26

The three of them decided it would just be best to admit what they had been doing and accept their punishment.

Bev reluctantly went to the door, opened it, and told Mrs. Beard, "We're ready to talk now."

Mrs. Beard came back in, quietly closed the door and took her seat at the desk. She leaned back in the chair, crossed her arms, and said, "Well, ladies. What do you have to tell me?"

As is often the case, parents know a lot more that goes on in a teenager's life than what the teen expects. The teens forget that the town is small, people talk and parents know other parents. Mrs. Beard already had a pretty good idea what had been going on. Additionally, one of the sales clerks from the *Montgomery Ward* store was getting suspicious and had contacted the home.

Sandy took over as spokesperson for the group. She explained how they would go into the "Wards" store, wearing clothes that were a little on the big side, and then slip tighter clothing on underneath. Sometimes only one girl would go in, sometimes two of the girls, and occasionally, all three would work together. Anticipating Mrs. Beard's next question, Sandy said, "And, no, none of the other girls are involved in this."

Mrs. Beard went on to tell them that this was disturbing. "You girls know better than to steal. Furthermore, you have caused embarrassment to the home. A lot of businessman make donations to the home. They will not appreciate hearing about this. Your punishment is going to be severe this time."

The girls were required to return the items to Wards, even though they had been worn. Each of them had to write a letter of apology to the store. In addition to being grounded for a month, they were assigned extra cleaning duties for a month at the home. For several weeks after, Mrs. Beard made a big deal out of examining the girls' clothing when they came home from school. The girls found this humiliating, which was Mrs. Beard's point.

As usual, an announcement was made the next morning at breakfast. Mrs. Beard told all of us what the three girls had done, further humiliating the girls. Mrs. Beard made them apologize to the group for the embarrassment they had brought to the kids at the home.

Later that day, I made some notes to myself:

- House parents, and parents, notice more than what we think they do.
- Parents and adults, just like us kids, "stick together." "Us against them," remember?

- Learn to make up better stories to tell adults.
- "Cover your tracks" before you commit the crime.
- Don't use other people's names in a lie.

I tucked these notes away in my strongbox for future reference, both as a teenager and as a parent.

Chapter 4
"BOYS WILL BE BOYS"

A nnie Volkstra was a college student from Oklahoma. She was a senior at the University of Oklahoma and was working at the home for a year. She had run out of money and had to take a year off. Her sociology professor, who attended a nearby Free Methodist Church, had seen an advertisement in the church bulletin for a position as a house parent at the Woodstock Children's Home. Her professor felt that this would be a valuable experience for her as she was studying to become a social worker. Annie applied and got the job.

Annie was not much older than some of us. She was pretty. She had red curly hair, cute freckles, a nice smile and large breasts. Besides being attractive, Annie was just a very pleasant person, always in a good mood. You could tell that she liked children. I'm sure she went on to have a good career in social work. One of her duties was to help us with our homework. All of a sudden, a lot of the boys showed more interest in their schoolwork and seemed to need extra tutoring from Annie.

Another one of Annie's duties was to serve as a night proctor at the main building of the home. She had her own room, located between the two boys' dorms. The room was small, but had a private toilet and sink, windows and two doors. One door opened into the younger boys' dorm and the other into the older boys' dorm. Of course these doors were always locked for her privacy. I don't know how she was able to live in that small room with all the commotion of about 10 boys on each side of the room. Fortunately, she liked to read and she seemed to have a lot of patience with the boys.

Sometimes during the night if a boy was sick or if we were having pillow fights, or if we were just causing general mayhem, Annie had to come into our dorms. She was usually dressed in her pajamas and robe, but would once in a while forget the robe and come out in her shorty pajamas. We all liked that. She probably wondered why we seemed to listen more attentively on some occasions than on others.

One boy, Scott, became kind of obsessed with his boyhood crush on Annie. Apparently, he had somehow got a glimpse of Annie in her bra and panties, although he never did disclose how. I assume he probably was looking through the keyhole in the door. The door used an old fashioned skeleton key and those keyholes were fairly large.

Scott was kind of a junk collector. He would always pick up things on the way home from school that he would put in his locker in the basement. Small hand tools, wire, old electrical outlets, and guess what? A key ring that someone had lost or discarded that had a skeleton key on it.

One weekend Annie went home to Norman, Oklahoma to visit her parents. Scott had shared his plan with a couple of us boys. He was going to see if his newfound skeleton key would unlock her door. His goal was to get his hands on one of Annie's bras. He wasn't going to keep it as a souvenir or anything like that, he just wanted to see her private clothing items. He also felt that this would give him some real bragging rights in the dorm since he knew all of us liked Annie.

It was a Saturday morning. Breakfast was over. The daily chores had been completed by the boys and most of them were in the recreation room of the main building, located beneath the younger boys' dormitory. We were watching cartoons on TV.

32

The "rec room" was large, with wood paneling on the walls and a linoleum floor that we constantly had to sweep, mop and wax. It contained one of the two televisions in the entire building. The other was in the formal living room on the other side of the building. That room and television were reserved for when children had company and for other special occasions. It was also the only room in the entire building with carpeting.

All of a sudden there was this loud noise. THUNK! Someone had dropped something upstairs in the dorm. The sound of wood against wood and a chinging sound like maybe a set of keys on wood alerted Mr. Wiser, a local man from the church who was not a regular house parent. He was helping out over the weekend while Annie was away. We always liked when this happened. It was like having a substitute teacher at school. It was always fun trying to get away with more mischief than usual. These people didn't know all the rules and it was easy to "pull the wool over their eyes." These "substitutes" generally were nice people that tried to be our friends.

Mr. Wiser immediately climbed the stairway leading up to the dorm, thinking that there may have been an accident or that someone got hurt. There was an accident alright. He

33

found Scott, lying on the floor, apparently unharmed, with a whole drawer of Annie's lingerie on his lap and the key ring with the skeleton key on the floor next to him. In his excitement, Scott had tripped while attempting to remove the drawer from the dresser. He fell over the end of the bed and landed on his backside in the doorway. By this time, all of the boys from downstairs had come up to the dorm to see what all the noise was about. Everyone had a pretty good laugh. They also got a good peek into that drawer, which added to the excitement of the situation.

Turned out that Mr. Wiser's name fit him well. After making sure that Scott was unharmed, he instructed each boy to sit quietly on his own bed. Scott was made to return the dresser drawer to its rightful place in Annie's room. He had to turn his beloved keys over to Mr. Wiser. Mr. Wiser then gave us all a lecture–first about "breaking & entering," and then about the appropriate way to treat girls. He said that we were at an age where we were becoming interested in girls and that was healthy. He said that in time we would all learn the "facts of life," but we needed to take our time and just let these things happen naturally. "You do not force your affections on girls," he said. And it is certainly wrong to commit a "crime" to get a girl's attention.

Scott had to spend the day alone in the dorm, but he had something to do though. Mr. Wiser instructed Scott to write an essay on what he had done wrong and what would have been a better way to approach Annie about his feelings. He was also required to write a letter of apology to Ms. Volkstra. This was the hardest part; he was so embarrassed about what he had done. She was going to think he was such an idiot! He hoped Annie wouldn't be angry with him.

I don't know if this caper was reported to anyone else at the home or not. Nothing else was ever said about it by the regular house parents. But I did notice a new lock on Annie's door the next week. Maybe it was just a coincidence? Hmmm. We also noticed that Annie never came into our dorm in those shorty pajamas anymore. Boy, Scott had ruined it for all of us.

After a couple of months, Annie returned to Oklahoma. I got a note from her one time after she graduated. She got a job with the Department of Human Services in her area. She wished me well. She didn't mention Scott. I showed him the note. I could tell that he was jealous. I let him have the note. You could smell her perfume on the paper.

Each of us was given a copy of the essay that Scott had been required to write. I still have a copy of it in my strongbox. Attached to it with scotch tape and string is a brass skeleton key. The key was not the one Scott had, but one I found one day while on my paper route. I will probably never use the key for anything, but I may read the essay from time to time as a reminder of how I should act appropriately with girls.

There are hardly any doors today that use a skeleton key, but I have kept it, "just in case."

Chapter 5

HOMEWORK

There were not a lot of exemplary students at the home. The home knew that most of us would not be going to college. We felt they just wanted us to get through school and graduate. I have to give them credit though. They did hire people to help us during the home's study hall four evenings a week, which were held in the dining room of the Harrison House, the residence for teens. These people were usually teachers from the local schools looking for part-time work.

Robin was one of the exceptions. She was one of the few students who made the honor roll. She was bright and worked hard at learning. She was also helpful to other kids with their school work. We were all jealous of her at report card time because of the accolades she received by house parents.

It was January and nearing the end of the first semester at school. One of the high school teachers, Mr. Ditka, taught history. He decided to give a test with an unusual twist. It was a long test and required detailed answers. The good news was that it was an "open book" test. There were three kids from the home that were in that American History class. Robin was in that class and everyone knew that she would "ace" the test, especially since it was open book. All three students worked on their test during that evening's study period. Robin completed her test during the required study period. Dave had to stay a little longer than the usual, but did complete it.

Christine, however, did not fare as well. She gave up half way through, as was her usual way of doing things. She told the study hall teacher, Mr. Nichols, that she was not feeling well. She promised that she would finish the test in her study hall during second period the following morning. The study hall teacher provided by the home went along with her program. He really had no responsibility to see that her work was done. He was just there to help. He told Christine, "Just make sure you get it turned in on time. I don't want Mr. Ditka to blame me."

Robin and Christine were roommates. While Robin was sleeping, Christine conjured up a plan. Even though the room was dark, Christine knew exactly where Robin had left her test paper. Christine quietly went to Robin's side of the room and removed the test from her nightstand. With flashlight in hand, she went to the bathroom, with a blanket, and made herself comfortable on the floor. (Hopefully, no one would need to use the toilet during the night).

Christine spent over an hour on the bathroom floor and copied Robin's test paper perfectly. She acted so proud of herself when she turned the test paper in the next day to Mr. Ditka. The paper was complete and Christine knew she would get at least a "B" if not an "A" and no one would be the wiser. She asked Mr. Ditka to let Mr. Nichols know that she had turned in the test.

This was a fairly typical way that Christine operated. She was generally cutting corners and looking for ways to shirk her responsibilities. She was not ambitious about anything. She was all about having a good time. This time, though, she really worked hard. She had stayed up late, lain on that cold bathroom floor and got the job done. She was so diligent with her copying that she even copied Robin's name and put it on her paper!

Christine didn't realize it, but Mr. Ditka noticed right away that Robin's name was on Christine's test paper. He just said, "Thank you, Christine," and took the paper. What Robin got back from Mr. Ditka was sheet of paper that was nearly blank. On it, at the top in bold red ink, "F." And two words written neatly underneath that said, "Nice try."

Christine almost broke out in tears. She was terrified. She figured she would be kicked out of school. Getting kicked out of school was a big "No -no" at the home. She would be grounded again. Christine was also upset with herself that she had betrayed her friendship with Robin. Robin would probably never trust her again. That was not a good situation with two people rooming together.

That night during study period, the current house parent, Mr. Newton, handed out a copy of the "Nice Try" paper that Christine had received from Mr. Ditka. He then lectured us about cheating in school. He said, "If you are going to cheat in school, you are probably going to cheat in life."

Christine was made to apologize to Mr. Nichols, and also to Robin, although she had already apologized profusely to Robin that day after school. Robin had been gracious and said, "Just don't let it happen again, but stay on your own side of the room."

Christine was required to take the test again. She had to do it in the school's detention area, after school. It took her three sessions to complete it. When she finally got it done, she got a "C-" on the test. She was disappointed, but that's the kind of grades she generally got.

Additionally, she got two weeks of detention from the school and was grounded by the home for the same two-week period. Mr. Nichol had told Christine that anyone caught cheating would usually be expelled, but she wasn't because Mr. Ditka had stuck up for her. Mr. Nichol also said, "But Mr. Ditka doesn't want anyone to know he went to bat for you He doesn't want to spoil his tough guy persona."

I kept a copy of the test and put it in my strongbox. Who knows? I may need it one day. I would probably have to take Mr. Ditka's class next year myself. I also kept a copy of Mr. Ditka's note, "Nice Try," as a reminder that cutting corners in life may not be a good idea after all. There were right ways to do things and cheating was not one of them.

Robin, by the way, went on to college and became a local teacher. Christine did graduate from high school, but in another state, where she had been reunited with her family. Hopefully, this cheating episode taught her a valuable lesson.

Chapter 6

MIDNIGHT RIDER

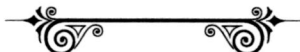

N ick was what we called a "gearhead." He loved cars. Every chance he got he would raise the hood of a car and admire the engine, and when he could, would tinker with it. Cars were all he ever talked about. Old cars, new cars, junk cars–he loved them all. He was always picking up used copies of auto magazines that people or businesses would dispose of. He would stop by *Reichert's Chevrolet*, on Clay Street, on the way home from school just to look at the new and used cars on their lot. He hoped he could get a job there someday.

Roger and Betty Emerson lived across the highway from the home. They owned a 1949 Ford convertible. It was a light yellow color with a white convertible top. It was a really cool looking automobile, I have to admit. Roger didn't drive the car a lot. He worked in a bank in Chicago and walked to the Chicago & Northwestern train station each day to commute to the city.

Occasionally, while Roger was working on his car, Nick would wander over to their house and visit. Sometimes Roger would let Nick sit in the car, "tinker" under the hood or help wash and wax the vehicle.

While working on the car, Mr. Emerson liked to share stories about Sherlock Holmes episodes from TV, as he was a big fan of the detective. Nick and Mr. Emerson both loved that car, but Nick was not fascinated with the detective stories. I think Nick and Mr. Emerson kind of tolerated each other, but did seem to have some rapport.

Nick just couldn't get that 1949 Ford out of his mind. He loved that car. One night, just after midnight, Nick snuck out of the dorm and stealthily walked over to the Emerson's house. Being summertime, the car had been left on the driveway overnight. There was a detached garage located behind the house, but Mr. Emerson seldom used it during the summer months. Nick was careful not to walk there directly. He skittered behind trees to avoid being seen. There was a curfew in town and he certainly didn't want to be caught and returned to the home in the middle of the night.

Nick approached the car and couldn't believe his luck. The convertible was unlocked. This was the 1950's and people didn't lock their house doors, much less their car doors. He looked across the street where the main building of the children's home sat. No lights were on and all was quiet. Nick quietly opened the driver's side door and slid into the seat. He closed the door very carefully.

He was lucky that the car was unlocked, but not lucky enough to have the keys left in it. No problem. Nick knew how to hot wire a car. He had been around enough cars and read enough car magazines that there wasn't much he couldn't do with an auto.

Just as he went to work on starting the car, he noticed something on the floor mat. He picked it up. A rabbit's foot on a key chain (no key though). A rabbit's foot–that meant good luck, didn't it? He put it in his pocket.

Nick rubbed the appropriate wires together, got a spark. The engine sputtered a little and finally started. He hoped Mr. Emerson didn't hear the sound. He backed out of the driveway onto Seminary Avenue (Route 47) and headed north. He went about a mile, passed the *Dog-n-Suds* drive-in and turned left on to Beech Ave. He then turned right on to Madison.

"Wow, this is so cool!" he said to himself. He looked in the rearview mirror to make sure he wasn't being followed. He continued on down to Willow Avenue and turned right. Another block and he came back to Route 47. He turned left, accelerated sharply, shifted and hit second gear. He depressed the accelerator more–and that's when he saw the flashing lights in his rear view mirror. Nick nearly peed his pants, but he pulled over to the side of the road. He couldn't turn the car off because he didn't have the keys to restart it. The police car had pulled off the road and parked behind Nick.

Officer Fyfe stepped out of his car, straightened his hat, tucked in his shirt and stood erect. He came to the window and asked for Nick's "license and registration." Nick had to admit that he did not have either one, and admitted, "I am only 15."

Officer Fyfe asked if this was his dad's car. Nick responded, "No, I just borrowed it from a friend."

"Wow, said officer Fyfe, must be a really good friend."

Officer Fyfe then instructed Nick to turn off the engine, lock the car and join him in the squad car. "We are going to the station, son," the officer said. Now Nick was really scared. Was he going to spend the night in jail? He hadn't really "stolen" the car. He just wanted to take it for a short ride and was then going to return it to Mr. Emerson's driveway.

By the time they got to the police station, Nick had come clean. He told Officer Fyfe that he lived at the children's home and that he had snuck out, hot wired the car and taken it for a ride. He explained that Mr. Emerson was a friend, although Nick had not asked for permission to "borrow" the car.

Officer Fyfe took him to the station, filled out a report and made sure that Nick got a good view of the jail cells. One of the cells held a drunk who was snoring and smelled badly of booze. The other cell held a man who looked like he had been in a fight. He had a black eye and blood was oozing from his lower lip. Nick sure did not want to spend the night there.

Officer Fyfe called the children's home. It took a while for Mr. Dodge to answer the phone. It was now almost 2:00 in the morning and the phone was in the office, two rooms away from the house parent's bedroom. Mr. Dodge told the policeman that he would "come right down," but Officer Fyfe told him he would bring Nick back to the home. Officer Fyfe thought the more time that Nick spent with the police, the more he would be intimidated. He was right. Nick really was scared. He was not only scared by the jail itself, but what was going to happen when he was returned to the home.

After the return of Nick and an explanation of the night's events, Officer Fyfe, Mr. Dodge and Nick all walked down to Mr. Emerson's. They knocked on the door, and after a bit, Mr. Emerson, in his robe and slippers, opened the front door. He hardly even noticed the policeman, the house parent or Nick. His eyes went right to the driveway.

He half shouted, "Where is my car?"

Officer Fyfe again explained the events of the past two hours, told Mr. Emerson where he could find his car and offered to give him a ride to get it. He then said, "Right now we are going to get this young hooligan to bed and we will sort all of this out in the morning."

Mr. Emerson had a daughter, Debi, a pretty girl and a year younger than me. She had dark hair and an infectious smile. She was home a lot when Nick was helping her dad. Debi's mom was always keeping an eye out though. She wasn't sure she liked how Nick was always looking at her daughter.

Mr. Emerson had always wanted a son as well. He rather liked Nick and enjoyed his visits while working on his car. Being the kind man that he was, he did not press charges against Nick.

He let Nick know that he was a bit disappointed in his actions and asked, "Why didn't you just ask me if you could drive the car?" Nick didn't know what to say. He felt pretty stupid for what he had done.

Mr. Emerson actually volunteered to be kind of a "mentor" to Nick. Mrs. Emerson was a bit wary. She wasn't used to having a teenage boy around. Roger allowed Nick to use the car to get his driver's permit, as Nick had recently passed Driver's Education at school and would be turning sixteen in a few days.

I later learned that Mr. Emerson was a little bit chagrined that he had not had the chance to solve the mystery himself of who had "stolen" his beloved car. He would have liked the chance to hone those detective skills of Sherlock Holmes that he so admired.

The home, however, was not as kind as Mr. Emerson. Nick thought he would be getting his driver's license in a few days, but the home's director, Mr. Redding, told him that he would have to wait 90 days. "Man, thought Nick, that is the worst punishment ever! I just went for a ride. I really didn't steal the car."

Nick and Mr. Emerson became good buddies. I actually think Nick took a little interest in their pretty daughter, Debi. He sure seemed to spend a lot of time over there. Maybe he would be able to take her to the drive-in in McHenry one night. He would have to put the convertible top up though.

After three months, Nick got his driver's license and eventually got a job working at the gas station/auto repair shop located about a mile down on Route 47, across from the former Hinner Bottling Co. Hank Schroeder was the owner of the station.

In addition to all those car magazines, Nick also collected key chains. He had two that had a rabbit's foot on them. Nick gave me one while we roomed together for a short time. I am not sure if it is the actual key ring he found in Mr. Emerson's car, but I gladly accepted it and put it in my strongbox. I hope it brings me more luck than it brought Nick that night. I attached this old skeleton key to it that I had found.

It's too bad that Nick hadn't found that funny hat that Mr. Emerson had–the one that looked like the hat Sherlock Holmes wore. I would have loved to put that in my strongbox.

Chapter 7

GROWING BOYS GET HUNGRY

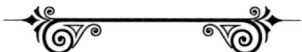

I am always hungry. Not starving, like a homeless person, just hungry. The house parents say it is because, "You are a growing boy." That is true–my pants are always too short. But that excuse doesn't help. We are not allowed to raid the refrigerator like my friends are allowed to do when they return home from school. I love it, when on occasion, I am allowed to go to a friend's house after school. There is always an abundance of food and snacks available. That isn't practical here at the home. If we were to do that, there wouldn't be enough food for dinner. Since we are discouraged from carrying cash, we can't even stop at stores on the way home from school to buy candy, pop or chips. So I am always, "just hungry." It seems that I am always scavenging for food.

It is about 3:00 in the morning. Denny and I are awake. We had been waking up about this time for several nights in a row. It was like we had set an alarm clock or something. We had a mission to accomplish, a caper that we had successfully enacted several nights in a row. I am using my considerable detective skills to commit a crime, not solve a crime this time Our mission was secret and we wanted to keep it that way. We didn't want to spoil a good thing by getting caught or maybe even worse, having to share our bounty.

There was a pantry located just off the large kitchen of the main building. It was stocked with canned goods and staples such as rice, noodles, flour and sugar. There was always a box of hard candy in there, but the pieces were always stuck together. It also had cookies! There was a milk machine that held several gallon containers of cold milk located in the dining room, just outside the front door of the kitchen. The lure of the combination of these two was too great for us two hungry boys.

The dorm we slept in had 14 beds. It was just one large room. There was another dorm just like it on the other side of the night proctor's room located between the two dorms. There was a lighted "exit" sign above the night proctor's door, which gave just enough light for the boys to get up during the night and use the bathroom. It also gave enough light to guide us to the stairway which would lead us to the first floor, to the kitchen and then to the pantry. We had to be careful here though. The top of the stairs was just a few feet away from the night proctor's door.

We knew those stairs well. We knew which ones creaked, so we would step over those. We were always careful to walk on the outside of the steps to avoid making more noise. There were doors at the top and the bottom of the stairway. There was a landing after a few steps and then the stairs turned left. There was a window in the wall at that point. The door at the bottom led into the recreation room, the most used room in the building, where we would read, play and watch TV.

Oh, an interesting note here. When watching TV, if a commercial comes on for beer or cigarettes, the house parent stands in front of the television so we can't see it. I like the Tareyton commercial–the guy with the black eye that says, "I would rather fight than switch." I think everyone likes the "Hamm's Bear" in the beer commercial. But I digress.

We made it down the stairs, across the "rec" room, through the door that connected to the back porch, and then an immediate right turn led us into the kitchen. Denny and I felt like cat burglars, except we were not dressed all in black.

We were getting so good at this. We could probably do it with our eyes closed now–exit light or not. We were amazed that none of the other boys ever heard us getting up in the wee hours of the morning.

The kitchen was large. It was more like a kitchen you would see in a fancy restaurant. A large icebox that was green and had six hinged doors on it. It seemed ancient, but it did the job. A big white refrigerator, stainless steel sinks that would accommodate large pans and cooking utensils. Fortunately, the girls had to help with the kitchen chores, so us boys didn't have to handle washing the huge pots and pans. The stainless steel stove had an abundant number of burners on it, with cooking ovens located beneath it. There was a long wooden counter than ran almost the whole length of one side of the kitchen. In the middle of the kitchen were two tables that were used for food preparation. Just on the other side of the pantry was the door leading to the basement, where we had to peel potatoes and deal with the rats (I really hated that chore!) In addition to the freezer in the kitchen, there was a huge walk-in freezer located off the porch that connected to the kitchen. Kids were always afraid of getting locked in there and freezing to death.

We slid into the kitchen and gently closed the door. "Now, that's strange," I said to Denny. Someone had left a light on in the pantry. It was almost like someone had been considerate and left the light on for us. It turned out that someone had.

We entered the pantry and saw why someone had really left the light on. "Aunt Lil," the cook, was sitting on a chair in there reading a book. She said, "Hello, boys. I have been waiting for you."

Aunt Lil was liked by all the kids. A very nice lady, always friendly and smiling. She had a son of her own. His name was Wayne and they lived in a cottage right off the back porch. (Yes, the same cottage where my strongbox is stowed away). She would invite us boys over to her place on either Friday or Saturday nights to have popcorn and watch *Shock Theater*. The band on the show was called *Marvin and the Deadbeats*. We were always a little apprehensive going back to our dorms. None of us wanted to admit we were frightened after watching the scary movie. We watched warily as we ran between buildings.

Aunt Lil said she had noticed that the cookies seemed to be mysteriously disappearing all of a sudden. She said she started keeping track and figured that someone had been taking them. Aunt Lil was a light sleeper and had decided to keep an eye on the kitchen during the night. Two nights in a row she had noticed the pantry light on. The second night she actually saw Denny and me leave the pantry.

Aunt Lil said, "You boys thought you were so clever. But it's pretty hard to fool me. I have a son of my own, you know. Not much gets by me." Aunt Lil scolded us and told us to never do this again or she would have to report us to our house parents. She then said, "Have your cookies and milk and go back to bed."

We were happy that we were not punished. That almost never happened at the home. We were somewhat embarrassed that we had been outsmarted by Aunt Lil. And we were more than a little worried that word might get back to Miss Campbell about our nightly escapade. Miss Campbell was a pretty lady, but was very strict. We agreed that in the future we would just have to live with waking up in the wee hours wanting a snack.

I don't know how long cookies will keep. On our way out of the pantry, I absconded a small, sealed bag of chocolate chip cookies (my favorite) to keep for another night. That was pretty dumb on my part. If Aunt Lil had seen that she probably would have lost that cool demeanor she had displayed. I didn't eat them. Instead, I wrapped them in some wax paper and later put them in my strongbox. I didn't really plan on eating them. (Denny would have if he ever found them–Denny would eat anything).

The cookies remained in the box to serve as a reminder to me. You are never as clever as you think you are. Someone is always going to find you out. I also learned that some adults are more understanding than we think. Aunt Lil understood that boys just get hungry.

Chapter 8
CONTRABAND

No smoking. If there was one rule the home and church really bore into us kids was that smoking was the number one, in their minds, of the deadly sins we could commit. No one who smoked was going to get into heaven. Smoking was the beginning to a life of crime and debauchery.

We were required to make our own beds daily. I didn't mind this, but a lot of the kids just hated making their beds. I remember Steve Homrig complaining, "Jeez, I just wish I could jump out of bed and leave it for my mom to make, like when I lived in my real home." House parents would check our areas almost daily for cleanliness and neatness. Every Saturday morning, ritual inspections were made of our foot lockers, drawers and under our beds. We also had to "change sheets" each Saturday. The bottom sheet went to the laundry and the top sheet was transferred to the bottom. I never understood this. Don't both sheets get dirty?

Every once in a while, however, a more thorough inspection was done. Mattresses were turned over, furniture was moved, drawers were emptied out. Some of the boys had pretty good hiding places for their personal belongings. With 14 boys, things had a way of "walking away" sometimes. One boy had discovered a loose floor board under his bed. With a knife, he was able to get it loose and he would hide things under the floor. Another boy actually cut a hole in the bottom of his mattress. I, of course, had my strongbox. Luckily, no one was able to inspect that. If they had, there would have been definite questions about the assortment of items found there.

There were two small closets in our dorm. One closet just had some poles for hanging clothes, where each of us had a section to hang our better clothes. Did I say "better" clothes? Those were our "Sunday" clothes that were saved to wear to church. The other closet had hanging space as well, but also had some "cubbyholes," about 15" x 15" that were assigned to each boy. The cubbyholes were mainly filled with toys–Lincoln logs, Erector sets, barn animals, baseball gloves and board games. It gave us a little extra storage room beyond our foot lockers.

The top shelves of the closet were too high for any of us to reach. We needed a ladder or a step stool to reach the top, so they were seldom used by us. The house parents would sometimes store things on the top shelves. They were allowed to search our storage areas, but theirs were strictly "hands off."

One Saturday morning, during breakfast, an announcement was made. Breakfast was the usual time for announcements–introductions of new kids or staff, schedule changes, and of course, "new rules". Today's announcement was that there would be a broad and thorough inspection of the boys dorms, immediately following breakfast. That didn't leave much time for anyone to do additional clean up or try to hide something he did not want found. Breakfast was quiet that morning. Everyone ate quickly. All the boys were busy thinking about whether they had any incriminating items to be found. Immediately following breakfast, all of us made a beeline to our dorms.

During the inspection, I heard our house father, Mr. Hopkins, exclaim, "What are these doing here? Who do they belong to?" A pack of opened cigarettes was found! Oh no! Someone was in major doo-doo. It was found on the top shelf of the closet next to the stairway. The pack was in a box filled with hangers, towels and washcloths. It looked as though the box might have belonged to a house parent. Could it be? Maybe one of the boys hid them there thinking they would never be found. It would have been difficult, though not impossible, for one or two of the boys to get the pack of cigarettes up there, but we could be pretty creative when we put our minds to it.

Upon further inspection of the box, it was discovered that some papers were used to line the bottom of the cardboard container–some newspapers and old wrapping paper. One of the pieces of paper was an envelope addressed to a part-time house parent, Colleen Bates. That lady just happened to be away for the weekend and was not aware of the inspection. Why had Mr. Hopkins even looked in that box? He must have gotten carried away. (I was the detective, why didn't he ask for my help)?

Mr. Hopkins did his best try to find out who the cigarettes belonged to. He questioned each boy individually and even threatened to punish all of us if someone did not admit to being the owner of the contraband. Finally, he gave up. He knew he would have to question Miss Bates upon her return. He would go from there.

60

Upon her return, Miss Bates (Ms. was not used back then) was confronted by the House Parent Supervisor about the pack of cigarettes. While Miss Bates did not want to admit that she was a "closet smoker," she also did not want for any of the boys to be suspected of smoking. Being a Christian young lady, she also did not want to lie. She admitted they were hers and that, indeed, she sometimes sneaked a smoke. This was the 1950's and most adults smoked, unless you were a member of the Free Methodist Church.

Miss Bates was only working at the home for the summer. She was serving an internship for one of her college classes. Fortunately for Miss Bates her summer internship at the home was going to be over in two weeks. She was allowed to stay on for that time.

She was a nice young woman who was good to the kids. She would sometimes take us in her car to the Dairy Queen for ice cream cones. We liked her car. It was an old "woody" station wagon. It was a long car, with wood paneling that ran along both sides. The brown color had faded badly. She even played softball with the boys. The girls liked her too. She would talk to them about boys and help them fix their hair. Even on her days off, Miss Bates would spend time with us.

I think Miss Bates's last two weeks at the home were long ones. The other staff members just didn't treat her quite the same after she admitted to her grave sin of smoking. I would see her sitting by herself in the lounge where the house parents sometimes congregated. I felt bad for her. She should not have been ostracized that way.

The house parent who had originally confiscated the cigarettes foolishly tossed them in the garbage can by the back door. Duh! With all these boys around, didn't he realize one of us was going to retrieve them? Well, I did. They went in my strongbox. That was handy. My strongbox was in the basement of the cottage, right by the garbage can.

Did those cigarettes start me on to the path of being a smoker? No, but they will serve as a reminder that we are all human. Adults, as well as children, sometimes have their secrets.

I am sure that if I get to heaven, I will see the pleasant Miss Bates. I doubt that either of us will have cigarettes up there, but I hope no one will be kept out of heaven just because they smoked or didn't make their bed daily.

Chapter 9
SPORTS SUNDAY

The children's home felt that Sunday was a day of rest. Go to church, have a nice Sunday dinner, a quiet afternoon and then church service again in the evening. Sunday dinners were right after church. We were required to remain dressed up. There would almost always be guests at the house parent's table. The executive director and his family usually ate there on Sunday. Many times there would be people from other areas that had come to the church that day and would be invited to have dinner at the home. We never knew if these visitors had an interest in the kids or if they were just looking for a free meal. Sunday dinner was always the best meal of the week, usually ham, roast beef or fried chicken.

Sunday was the primary day that kids had visitors. A lot of parents or relatives would drive to Woodstock for the afternoon and spend an hour or two with their offspring. Once in a while, the adults would take the child somewhere for a while, but most times the visits were just had at the home itself. Sadly, a lot of the kids would be moody after these visits. So many parents would make false promises about getting the kids out of the home. A lot of disappointment.

We were not allowed to go to the store on Sundays. A "rest hour" was enforced every Sunday afternoon from 3–4:00. We had to stay in our rooms and be quiet. Sunday evening dinner was always light. Cold cereal or white rice with raisins (yuk) were pretty normal. Nor were we allowed to participate in organized sports on Sunday.

Bill was in eighth grade at Clarence Olson School. He was quarterback on the football team, which won the conference that year. He was big for his age and was a pretty good athlete. He loved sports. He was on the football team, basketball team and played "Teener League" Baseball. He carried a basketball, bat and baseball mitt with him on his bike–always looking for a "pick-up" game.

On one autumn Sunday, during the noon dinner, Bill got a phone call. That was unusual in itself. Phones were not everywhere then like they are now. Our telephone usage was pretty closely monitored. Cell phones didn't even exist. The phone numbers in town had just got their first prefix–338. We were making progress.

The caller was Frank Gates. Bill knew Mr. Gates from Teener League. Bill was on the Tigers and Mr. Gates coached one of the competing teams, the Dodgers. Bill Livengood and Wayne Sorenson played on that team. He was a hard driver, a good coach and seemed to be a real nice man. Mr. Gates asked Bill if he could come and play football that day for the "Bull Valley Bulldogs." Bill was unfamiliar with the team, but knew some of the kids that Mr. Gates mentioned. This prospect excited Bill, but he knew it wouldn't be allowed.

Bill told Mr. Gates that he would love to play, but was not allowed to play on Sunday. Mr. Gates asked if there was not some way around this. Bill thought a while and said, "Maybe there is." Bill suggested that he just be invited to one of the boy's homes for the afternoon. Mr. Gates or some other adult could just pick Bill up and bring him home later. No one would know the difference. The plan was put into action.

A while later, Mr. Starck, whose son, Jamie, played on the team, picked Bill up and delivered him to the place where the game was to be played. This worked out well. Bill had been to the Starck's home before. They had invited him to their home for Christmas day one time. Bill had to put on the uniform in the car.

The reason Mr. Gates had asked Bill to play was because they were playing a team from Wonder Lake. I don't recall the name of the team, but I do remember the name of their star player because Bill went on to high school with him. Bill would occasionally mention his name and talk about that game.

Their star player's name was Ed Green. Ed was also big for his age. He was strong, fast and talented. He was a year older than Bill. Bill's job that day was to play Ed one-on-one. Bill was supposed to keep him from scoring touchdowns. Easier said than done. Bill did his best, but was outplayed by Ed, who became a star football player at Woodstock High School. The Bull Valley Bulldogs lost the game.

Bill would have gotten away from this incident unscathed if he hadn't taken such a beating on the field. He had been spiked in his right leg, behind the shin, and had a pretty good cut to show for it. Also, his face was a little bruised. Bill was showing off his spiked leg to a couple of other boys, who were duly impressed. They got so engrossed in their conversation that they didn't realize that Mr. Horn, the house-parent, was standing on the other side of the partition that had recently been erected in an attempt to separate the bets a little so the large room wouldn't look so much like a dorm any longer.

Mr. Horn stepped into the area where the boys were reviewing the day's events and said, "What's all the excitement about? What happened to your leg, Bill? I thought you were just visiting your friend." Bill tried to make some excuses for his appearance.

Bill told Mr. Horn that he had "fallen off a bike" while they were horsing around. "Then we were playing some football with the neighbors." His excuses were useless. Mr. Horn picked up the item of clothing off the bed. It was a dirty football jersey. On it was imprinted, "Bull Valley Bulldogs" and the number "14." After the game, one of the parents had said, "Let Bill keep the jersey. He played hard today."

Bill's former houseparent, Mr. Gearhart, would probably have let the whole incident slide. He liked sports and encouraged Bill to play them. Mr. Gearhart also felt that having some of the boys from the home excelling in sports was a very positive thing for the home. Mr. Horn, however, was not a sports fan. He was more inclined towards music and was a bit of a bookworm. He was very pedantic in his ways. He told Bill that he did not believe Bill's story and was going to call Mr. Gates himself. "It looks to me like you were playing football, alright, but for a team, not just a friendly game of touch football." Bill finally admitted what he had done. He didn't want Mr. Gates or any other parents involved. These people had always been good to Bill.

Mr. Horn said, "You know you have broken the rules. You know how the home feels about playing organized sports on Sunday. You will have to be punished." Bill was grounded for the next four Sundays and was told that his activities would be monitored very closely from now on. He was also told that if this happened again, that Bill would be removed from whatever organized sport he was involved with at the time. Bill accepted the punishment and apologized for his deception, but he really could not understand why they couldn't play organized sports on Sundays. None of his friend's parents could fathom that either.

The next year Bill had a problem again with organized sports on Sunday. He was on the All-Star team in Teener League and one of the games was on a Sunday. The team had won their first two games and the next one was to be played on a Sunday, in Elgin, Il. If they won the first game at 12:00, they would play another at 4:00. Not only was it a problem playing on Sunday, but Bill would also have to miss church services. Jim Smith, Bill's coach, talked to the people at the home. It almost took a "dispensation from the pope" to allow him to play, but permission was finally granted. Too bad for all the fuss–Woodstock lost the first game and was eliminated from the tournament.

Bill later told me that maybe playing sports was going to be a bigger problem than he wanted to deal with. He loved playing sports of all kinds. It helped him make friends and he liked the physical aspect of it, but it seemed that it always was causing problems with scheduling, meals, laundry and having to get special permissions.

These special permissions did not go unnoticed by the other kids. Some of them were quite resentful. They felt that Bill was receiving special privileges when they were not. This was a little disconcerting to Bill. He felt he was doing a good thing by excelling at sports. He thought the home should have been happier. It was good "PR" for the home when any of the kids did well. But Bill cared about the other kids' feelings too.

Bill eventually made the decision to just give up sports. It was a hard decision and one he later told me, "was probably not a good one." He said that he never regretted being at the home. He was thankful, in fact, for the home, but he just couldn't understand why his involvement in sports had to cause such a problem.

It was on the same day, while Bill was in a kind of disconsolate mood, that he gave me the bulldog's jersey and said, "I guess I won't be needing this anymore. I want to forget about the episode. I am just going to put sports out of my mind. I need to find a job anyway. I need the money."

I have that jersey. I remember trying it on. It just didn't look the same on me. Bill always looked like a linebacker. I stored the jersey away in my strongbox, rather than wearing it.

I always felt bad about this whole situation. Bill was a good kid, liked sports and generally tried to abide by the home's rules. This was one of the situations where the rules at the home could have been a little more pliable to allow a boy to just have some fun.

Chapter 10

THE RUNAWAY

There were a fair amount of the kids who went through the home that ran away. Most were found and returned fairly quickly. A couple made it for a few days. Almost always, the kids headed straight for their parent's home, which made finding them pretty easy. One young man made it all the way to Texas, but was found and returned to the home. Most of the kids who did run away only did it once, but once in a while there was a repeat offender.

Travis came to the home when he was 14. He had already been in another children's home in Chicago and had been in two foster homes. He had run away from all three. His social worker from the court, Miss Shefner, told him that this was his last chance. If he ran away again he would be sent to a detention home for boys. His social worker assured Travis that he would not be able to run away from there.

Sure enough, Travis quickly became disenchanted with life at the children's home. One Saturday afternoon he asked for permission to visit a new friend he had made at school. The house parent told him he could. He would have to be home by five o'clock. Since it was now 1:00, that would give him a four-hour head start on his journey. He could be "long gone" by 5:00.

Travis walked south on Route 47, crossed Lake Avenue. Standing in front of Edgetown Bowling Alley, he put out his thumb. In those days a lot of people still hitch hiked. It wasn't considered nearly as dangerous as it is today. It didn't take long to get a ride. Two boys, probably 16 or 17 years of age, in a blue and white, 2-door, 1958 Chevrolet Belair pulled over and motioned him in. "Nice car—must be their parents," thought Travis.

"Where you headed?" asked the driver.

Travis shrugged his shoulders and said, "Anywhere away from here." The boy in the passenger seat asked Travis his name. Travis volunteered his name and asked theirs.

The driver said, "Our names aren't important. Just be glad you're getting a free ride."

The guy in the passenger seat, who was kind of scruffy looking, asked, "What are you running from?"

Travis told him that he was recently placed in a children's home and he didn't like it there. The driver, a cleaner-cut looking guy, and his buddy exchanged a funny glance with each other. The driver laughed a kind of snort and said, "I'll be darned. It's a small world."

They were proceeding down Route 47 toward Huntley. Travis was getting kind of an uneasy feeling in his stomach, thinking maybe he should have waited for another ride. These guys seemed to have an attitude that Travis found kind of intimidating. Maybe he shouldn't have thought about running away again. The other times he had run away sure hadn't turned out so well.

The scruffy guy in the passenger seat was playing with this Zippo lighter the whole time. Kept clicking the top open and closed. It had an insignia of a rifle on it. The guy could see Travis watching him. He said, "I don't smoke. I just like the gun on this thing. Came with the car." Travis was really feeling uneasy now.

At this point the driver told Travis that they were also runaways. They had just this morning run away from a children's home in Rockford, Illinois. They had hitch hiked all the way to Belvidere. That is where, he said, "We kind of borrowed this nice automobile." The smirk on his face told Travis that "borrowed" was a euphemism for "stolen." The driver said Travis was welcome to ride along with them to their destination, which was Chicago. "But that's it. We will get you their and dump you off. We aren't going to share our names. Don't want you to know too much. And if anyone asks about us, you just play dumb." The scruffy guy said roughly, "You got that?" Travis nodded his head in agreement.

Finally, they made their way to the toll way, that nice new roadway that had recently been built–connecting Chicago, Rockford and places beyond. They had been on the road for a while and were getting hungry. They decided to stop at the Des Plaines Oasis, which was located over the toll way. It had a lunch counter, restrooms, and sold maps, souvenirs and such to travelers. There was also a gas station on each side of the restaurant. The car was getting low on gas. The driver asked Travis if he had any money. Travis had about $15 in his pocket. He offered $5, which the driver gladly took. $5 bought a lot gas in those days. The attendant filled the tank, washed the windshield and checked the oil. The boys parked the car.

They were having hamburgers and fries at the McDonald's located within the Oasis and observing the other travelers coming and going. They were doing a little "girl watching" at the same time. Their eyes and attention were focused out the window. They didn't notice the two Illinois State Police patrolmen walking up to their table. One of the officers cleared his throat and said, "Hi fellows, where you headed?" He then asked for identification. The two boys from Rockford both had driver's licenses and handed them over. The taller, older cop said, "We thought that was you two. Now, who is this fine young man with you?"

Travis said, "My name is Travis, but we are not together. These guys were just kind enough to give me a ride."

The shorter, younger of the two officers told Travis, "Come with me," and took him to another table, while the taller officer took a seat with the Rockford boys at their table.

Travis was scared. He knew he had better tell the truth and face the consequences. These State Police Officers looked more official and a lot scarier than local policeman he had dealt with in the past. He gave his name, told the officer that he had run away from the Woodstock Children's Home that afternoon, and that he would be glad to get away from "those creepy guys. They are kind of scary."

The officer told Travis that they had been looking for the two of them. The boys had run away from a home in Rockford this morning and stole the car in Belvidere. The police were on the lookout for the boys and the car. The police had the license plate number. The boys were from Chicago and the police were pretty sure they would be heading there. The officers had just gotten lucky seeing the stolen car at the Oasis. They also had good descriptions of the boys.

The officer told Travis that he would have to contact the children's home. Travis knew that and he also knew what it meant. He had struck out this time. His social worker, Miss Shefner, had already warned him. He would probably be going to "Charlie Town."

The other officer let the boys from Rockford finish their meal. He then had them stand up. He handcuffed them and led them away. Travis couldn't believe they were handcuffed. Travis hoped they weren't going to do that to him. Travis figured the boys were handcuffed because of the auto theft. He guessed they would be going to jail.

As for Travis, he figured his next stop was "Charlie Town." That was the St. Charles Home for Boys, located in St. Charles, Illinois. A scary place. It was a detention home. It had a chain link fence around it, had guards instead of house parents, and had a reputation for being very strict. It was basically a jail for teenage boys. The kids at the home had heard stories about it. A couple of different teenage boys who came through the home had spent time there. It was not a place you wanted to be.

Travis was taken by the police, though not in handcuffs, back to the children's home. A couple of weeks later, on a Monday morning, he was being packed up to be transported to St. Charles by Miss Shefner and a police officer. Travis couldn't believe she had brought a police officer along. He wasn't a criminal. He had just run away, for crying out loud.

I was in his room that day. He looked sad and defeated. He couldn't believe how badly he had screwed up this time. He reached in his pocket and pulled out the Zippo lighter, with the gun on it. The boy in the car had set the lighter on the table at the Oasis. When the officers found them, the boy forgot about the lighter. Travis had picked it up and pocketed it. Travis tossed me the lighter and said, "I guess you might as well have this. Where I'm going, the guards will just steal it from me." He dejectedly walked away with his meager belongings.

I never saw or heard of Travis again. I hope he learned a lesson and straightened out. I hope they were not too cruel to him at "Charlie Town." Hopefully his stay there was brief. I hope he didn't try to run away again. Travis never seemed to be a bad guy. He didn't like being moved from home to home. He just wanted to go back and live with his parents in Chicago. He couldn't seem to realize that the more he ran away, the less likelihood there would be of that happening.

I would like to have carried that lighter around in my pocket. It was cool looking. Even though Travis said that the "scruffy guy" in the car gave him "the creeps," it was kind of a cool sound that the lighter made when you clicked the top open and closed.

Instead, I tucked the lighter with the rifle on it in my strongbox. Each time I saw it, it seemed to say to me, "Don't run away. It's not worth it."

Chapter 11

THE OLD LIBRARY STORY

One of the ways kids at the home got away in the evening, especially during the school year, was to use the excuse that they had "to go to the library." They would say they were doing a project or paper at school and could only get the research at the library. In those days, we didn't have the internet. We didn't even have fax machines yet. Copy machines had just been invented!

For some reason, the girls seemed to use this excuse a lot more than boys. And generally when a girl used the excuse, she needed to have another girl accompany her. This was good, I guess, as sometimes the girls would have to walk home in the dark. Other times, the house parent would take them and pick them up. That way, the house parent felt pretty sure that they were where they were supposed to be.

One particular Wednesday evening, Sharon and Carla had asked permission to go to the library to do research for a paper they were doing for Mr Radke's English Literature class. Permission was granted. It was a little cold and drizzly out that evening so Mr. Britton had said he would take them to the library. The library was open from 7–9:00 in the evening. He assured them he would be there at 9:00 to pick them up. The girls said they wouldn't mind walking, but Mr. Britton insisted.

Sharon and Carla got their books, spiral notebooks and pencils together. Mr. Britton took them to the library, arriving right at the time of opening. The library was a good place to go, whether to actually study or to meet friends. It was clean, warm and had good washrooms. The washrooms were important in case one needed to change clothes or put on perfume to cover the smell of cigarettes. Also, if you didn't talk too loud or cause a disturbance, you could pretty well come and go from the building as you liked. Plus, there were usually other kids from school to visit with.

Sharon and Carla had a plan. They had already arranged for Sharon's latest love interest, Bobby, to pick them up at 7:10. Bob was also going to bring along a friend who said he liked Carla. Bobby had just gotten a new Chevy Malibu and he was anxious to show it off. As soon as Mr. Britton left, Sharon and Carla had retreated to the washroom and put on some different clothing, which they thought was a little sexier. And, of course, they put on lipstick and make-up and touched up their hair. They didn't want to do this at the home because Mr. & Mrs. Britton would probably figure out what they were up to.

Carla, Sharon, Bobby and his friend, Jake, left in the car about 7:15. They rode around for a little while, got a root beer at the "A & W" drive-in on Washington Street, the one where that really hot girl, Cheri Mansfield, worked. Then they found a quiet road just north and west of town where they could enjoy themselves–just some laughs and a little necking. After all, this was Carla and Jake's first time together, although they had been flirting at school for a while. Time had passed quickly, which it always does under those circumstances. It was now 8:30. Bobby had just enough time to get the girls back to the library so they could change clothes, take off some make-up, cover the cigarette smell and prepare for Mr. Britton's arrival.

Bobby turned the ignition key. The engine just kind of groaned, but the car wouldn't start. He turned it again. It still wouldn't start. "Crap, said Bobby, we are dead meat." Bobby was really upset. "This is a brand new car—this shouldn't be happening," he grumbled, clearly embarrassed.

Jake said he would take a look under the hood. He said he was "pretty good with cars." Turns out that neither Bob nor Jake was good enough. They checked the battery, carburetor, spark plugs, distributor wires, everything they could think of. The car just would not start. It was getting later and later. The girls were really starting to worry. Finally, the guys gave up.

Jake walked to a nearby farm house. That was a little scary. He hoped there was no guard dog out in the yard or tractor parts to trip over. He walked up the rickety steps, crossed over the porch and knocked on the door. An older man, dressed in coveralls, who looked like he was ready for bed, answered the door. He looked Jake up and down and asked, "What can I do for you? You aren't selling something at this hour are you? You are aren't one of those Jehovah Witness people are you?"

Jake smiled that easy smile of his and said, "No, I am neither of those. Just had a little car trouble a bit down the road. My friend and I, and, uh, a couple of girls were just sitting in the car talking and now the car won't start."

The farmer said they could use his phone to call their parents. Jake said he would rather not do that. The farmer, a pretty smart old boy, said, "Let me take a look." He came out of the house and walked to his shed. He meandered out of the shed with a small toolbox and also a red metal gas can. Then it hit Jake! Jake just shook his head. He couldn't believe it. It now dawned on him what the problem was. They had run out of gas! He was supposed to remind Bobby to get some gas. In all the excitement, both boys had forgotten.

The farmer put the couple of gallons of gas he had in the tank and winked at Jake. The car started right up. Jake offered to pay the man for the gas. The man just snickered. "Keep your money. The show was worth it for me."

There was quite a discussion in the car. It was now 9:00 and Mr. Britton would be at the library. The girls knew they were in big trouble. They tried to think of a story they could make up that would sound legitimate. The real problem was, if they didn't get back to the home soon the house parents would call the police. That would cause more of a problem.

The four of them finally decided that the best course of action was just to go back to the home, tell the truth and face the music. Bobby and Jake told the girls they would talk to Mr. & Mrs. Britton and take the blame. They would tell the house parents that this was all the boys' idea. The girls would say they really did need to go to the library. They would say they just showed up and then they all decided to go for a root beer. Sharon and Carla appreciated their chivalry, but knew the Britton's wouldn't fall for it. They had been house parents too long and they weren't dumb either.

It was almost 9:30 by the time they got back to the home. Needless to say, the Britton's were livid. Mr. Britton had asked the librarian if she knew of the girls whereabouts. She said she had seen them leave the building about 7:15, "with some boys" and had not seen them since. Mr. & Mrs. Britton had put two and two together and figured out exactly what had transpired. By this time all of us other kids knew what was going on. News of this nature traveled very fast in the dorms. We were not surprised.

Before the four teens arrived in the parking lot outside the Harrison House, I had decided to get out my Polaroid camera. I wanted to savor the look on the girls faces when they were approached by the house parents. When the girls got out of the car, their faces were ashen and their eyes had a look like a feral cat caught in the headlights of a car. I walked up to the car and snapped their picture. The girls did not appreciate having their picture being taken at that time.

"You fink," Sharon yelled.

As hard as Bobby and Jake tried, the house parents just didn't fall for their story. The boys were told to leave. Mr. Britton said, "I will be calling both your parents." That had Bobby worried. His dad was pretty strict with him. Jake didn't figure his parents would care much about this. They were pretty easy-going. It would be different if there had been drinking involved.

Sharon and Carla received the usual lecture kids at the home got, about house parents not being able to trust the teens when they did things like this, what a sin it was to lie, and how "worried" the house parents were. The girls listened and acted like they truly felt remorseful. They really only felt bad because they got caught. Being with the boys even for that short time was worth it.

Both Sharon and Carla were grounded for a month. Phone privileges were revoked as well. If they needed to use the library, a teacher would have to call the home. In fact, Mr. Britton thought that might be a good policy from that day on for all library requests. This upset the girls. There was nothing worse in the minds of the teens than the whole group being made to suffer because of something that one or two kids had done.

Mr. Britton called the parents of the boys. He did not want local parents to think the home took this kind of behavior lightly. Bobby's dad didn't sound very pleased and told Mr. Britton, "I will deal with this."

Jake's mom took the call from Mr. Britton and simply said, "Thanks for calling."

I never heard what the parents of Bob and Jake did. I doubt their punishments were as severe. Most of the parents of friends from the home felt that the rules there were far too strict anyway. There were times when some parents of friends were even "in cahoots" with the kid's plans.

Although the girls didn't like me taking their picture and wanted me to give it to them so they could destroy it, I kept it. Another memento for my strong box. I attached a note to it, "Be more original. Don't use that old library story." I think every parent has heard that one at least once. I am pretty sure a lot of the parents had used it at one time or another themselves (maybe even Mr. & Mrs. Britton had too).

Chapter 12

THE CAR WASH

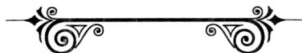

B rett was fifteen. He was a tall guy with a good physique. He was strong, with lots of energy. He had a hard time sitting still in church and in school. He liked to be busy. He was also one of those people who wanted to have friends. He was always trying to please people. He had a girlfriend, Michelle, from high school, but never had much money to take her anywhere. He mowed some lawns, washed some windows and things like that, but he needed something with a regular paycheck.

His best friend, Justin, worked at Rusty Johnsons' Car Wash, located just off the highway at Route 47 and Calhoun. Justin got him a job there. Perfect kind of job for Brett. It was physical, the hours worked well with his school schedule, he got to meet new people and he got to work with his best friend. He had to walk about a mile to the car wash and then another mile home each time he worked, but that didn't hurt him. The pay wasn't great, minimum wage, but he was only fifteen. Brett being a good worker, he figured he would get periodic raises.

Emptying the trash was always an experience. He couldn't believe what people would empty out of their cars. It seemed that people simply threw all their trash on the floor of the car and then used the car wash as their personal garbage service. Some people brought bags of trash from their homes. Sometimes people must have changed their clothes in the car, as there were lots of days when old clothes were found in the trash. The trash was always full of fast food wrappers, empty pop and beer bottles and even condoms. One time, Brett & Justin found a small dead dog that someone had thrown in the dumpster. Gross!

A lot of funny things happened at the car wash. One day when Justin was working, a very cute and shapely teenage girl had pulled into one of the bays. She got out of her car and approached Justin. He figured she needed change. She walked up to him and said, "Sir, could you help me take off my bra?"

Justin's teeth nearly fell out. He couldn't help himself. His eyes moved to her chest and he said, "Uh, well, yeah, I guess I could do that."

The girl, blushing, said, "Not that bra, silly, the one on the front of my car." Both young people were clearly embarrassed, but both laughed. Justin helped her take off the rubberized bra from the grill of her car. She gave him a dollar tip. Justin was reluctant to share this story with his girlfriend, Shannon, afraid she would be jealous, but he did tell her after all. Shannon just laughed at him and said, "Boys, you guys are all alike."

This was the early days of car washes. There were no "automatics" like today. People had to wash the cars themselves. They needed help learning how to use the equipment. Justin and Brett had to help people with that. Other responsibilities of the job included making change for customers, selling tokens, emptying the trash and keeping the property looking nice. Sometimes the guys would give a little extra help to people washing their cars, especially older people and young ladies.

Every once in a while the guys would get tips from people, which they were allowed to keep. Occasionally, people would forget to take their change or would carelessly drop coins.

The boys made a few extra bucks each week just by keeping their eyes open.

The car wash didn't have a cash register. Money was kept in a drawer in the office, along with a coffee can full of tokens that people could buy. A car wash generally cost $1.00 (four quarters). A person could buy five tokens for a dollar, thereby getting a little better pricing. All employees were on the "honor system." They were trusted to make correct change and sell tokens for the right amount. The owner would come in every day or so, collect the money and make a deposit.

One day Brett's girlfriend, Michelle, brought her parent's car in to wash. Brett, wanting to impress her, just gave her a few tokens and then helped her wash the car. Justin saw what happened and warned Brett that he shouldn't do that. "This is a small town. Word travels fast and the owner could find out," Justin warned him. Justin told Brett that he had gotten the job for Brett and didn't want to jeopardize his own employment.

Brett said, "Don't worry; Michelle would never tell anyone."

But Brett couldn't resist. He wanted people to like him. He began giving away tokens to friends at school. He figured the owner would never find out since he didn't keep good track of the tokens anyway, and Brett always told his friends that they shouldn't tell anyone that they got the tokens free.

Brett was having some problems in his geometry class. It was nearing the end of the semester and Brett thought he might even fail the class. One of his classmates, Craig Johnson, offered to give him some help just before a test. As a result, Brett did well on the test and passed the class. Brett said, "Hey, I appreciate your help. I'd like to give you these car wash tokens for your help." Craig tried to resist, but Brett insisted. Craig finally took the tokens. Unfortunately, Brett did not make the connection between Craig's last name and that of the car wash owner–"Johnson." Apparently, Craig was the nephew of Rusty Johnson, the car wash owner.

That Saturday when Brett showed up for work, Rusty Johnson was in the "office" area of the car wash. When Brett went into the office to "punch in, " Mr. Johnson stepped between him and the time clock. He handed Brett five tokens and said, "My nephew, Craig Johnson–I think you know him– gave me these. He said you gave them to him." Craig also had told Mr. Johnson that word was going around school that Brett had been giving tokens out to friends. Craig had confirmed this with two mutual friends.

Mr. Johnson told Brett that he was really disappointed in him. He asked if Justin was doing the same thing. Brett assured Mr. Johnson that Justin was not. Mr. Johnson told Brett that this was all very unfortunate because Brett was reliable, a hard worker and people liked him. He explained that Brett was stealing from him and would have to be punished.

Brett, now nearly in tears, said, "I understand. I apologize."

Brett felt really ashamed and frustrated. He had ruined a good thing. While he had tried to justify in his own mind that passing out the tokens wasn't really "stealing," deep down he knew it was. Now he was going to lose this job that he really liked. And who knew what punishment the home would provide? He sure hoped that Justin wasn't going to lose his job over this.

Rusty Johnson was a wise and nice man. He knew that Brett was a good, hard-working kid that just wanted too much to please people. Mr. Johnson felt bad for Brett that he lived at the children's home. He said to Brett, "Let's make a deal." Brett could keep his job, but he would have to work two weeks for nothing to repay for the tokens he had given away. Also, he would be required to wash and wax, by hand, Mr. Johnson's car and truck, weekly, for one month.

Mr. Johnson then gave Brett and Justin both a talk about honesty and the importance of integrity and hard work. Mr. Johnson was not a man who used fancy words, but he got his point across. Needless to say, Justin was not pleased that he had to listen to Mr. Johnson's rebuke and was even more upset with Brett for his actions. He told Brett that he would forgive him, but warned him that if it happened again, he would personally report it to Mr. Johnson and to the home. And it would be the end of their friendship.

The children's home never found out about this episode. It was difficult for Brett to get the money together to turn in his earnings for the next two weeks though. He had to work extra hard to earn tips and even had to borrow some money from Michelle. He didn't want to have to explain to the home why he didn't have the money even though he was working. Michelle wasn't real pleased either since Brett couldn't even afford to take her to a movie for a few weeks.

Brett had passed out a few tokens to some of us kids at the home. Obviously, we didn't need car washes, but the tokens were shiny, gold and silver, and kind of cool looking. I don't know what other kids did with the tokens, but mine went into my strongbox. They would serve as a reminder to me not to, "Bite the hand that feeds you." When someone is kind enough to give you a job, be thankful and respect them–do not steal from them. It also taught me that having a good friend is important. You need to respect them also.

There is an interesting side note to this story. I heard that years later, Brett and Justin started a car wash of their own in another town. I'll bet they devised a better system for keeping track of their tokens.

Chapter 13

"PEEPING TOM" (AND TIM)

There were three sets of twins at the home during my tenure there. They all shared one thing in common. They were constantly fighting with the other twin. But you didn't want to come between them–they would turn on you as one. There were two sets of male twins and a brother and sister who were twins.

Tim and Tom were one set of twins. They had no other siblings at the home. They were nice boys, a little immature for their age, in my opinion. At the time of this caper, they were 12 years old. They lived at the main building. The next year they would move to the Harrison House for teenagers.

Tim and Tom had been at a friend's house for the evening and were walking back to the home. Coming from town, they had to pass the teen residence before getting to the main building. It was dark. They had turned down Mansfield Avenue, which separated the main buildings from the Harrison House. They were going to take the gravel road that ran by the garden and chicken coop. They noticed a light come on and saw some movement in a window in the girl's dorm on the second story of the Harrison House.

The window was located at the top of the fire escape located on the north side of the building. They were curious. They had little knowledge of girls and their anatomy. This was 1960. There were not the kinds of ads or programs on TV that showed half-naked women like they do today. There were no sex education classes in those days. The boys were not perverts or anything, they just wanted to "take a peek."

They scaled the fire escape. Upon reaching the top they discovered the window was frosted over and was also locked. Just a circular latch for a lock. Tom had a pocket knife. He was able to push it through the crack and maneuver the part that turned in the base and get it unlocked. When they pulled the window out the circular portion fell to the ground. Oh well, probably no one would ever notice it anyway.

They peered into the open space for quite a while, but unfortunately, no girls appeared. They decided to wait a few minutes longer. Big mistake! They heard the sound of car tires crunching on gravel. Mr. Tracy parked his car right near the bottom of the fire escape. Why hadn't he parked under the carport, like he always did? The boys were really nervous, standing as still as they could, just hoping that Mr. Tracy would get into the building quickly.

Tom slipped his knife into his jeans pocket. At least he thought he had. But no, he had missed his pocket and the darn thing clanged all the way down the fire escape. Tom couldn't believe how loud the noise was. People probably heard the noise a half a mile away. At least it seemed that loud, under the circumstances.

Of course, Mr. Tracy heard the noise. He looked up and saw Tim and Tom. "You guys get down here, right now!" he yelled. They slowly worked their way down the fire escape.

Mr. Tracy asked them to explain what they were doing up there, even though he already had a pretty good idea. The twins just looked at each other. They were so scared they could barely speak. Mr. Tracy said, "All right then, we'll let the Hoovers deal with this." He walked them to the main building and turned them over to their own house parents, Mr. & Mrs. Hoover. The Hoovers were quite chagrined at learning what the boys had done. It was bad enough that they were late getting home, but the news about the window peeping really bothered them.

When Mr. Hoover asked what they thought they were doing, Tim exclaimed, "We were just curious. Man, we didn't even see anything and now we are in a load of trouble." Mr. Hoover asked the boys if they thought their actions were appropriate.

Tim responded, "No." Mrs. Hoover asked them if they would like the girls in the dorm to know what they had done. Tom responded, "Absolutely not." Mr. Hoover told the boys to go to bed and think about what they had done.

The twins didn't sleep very well that night. To be honest, the only reasons they regretted what they had done were that they "didn't see anything" and that they got caught in the act. What worried them more was what kind of punishment was waiting for them.

Breakfast lasted forever. It seemed that every time the boys looked up, Mr. and Mrs. Hoover were staring at them. Was it their imagination or were the girls looking at them differently? This was killing them! After breakfast, Mr. Hoover told Tim and Tom to come to the office.

Mr. Hoover gave the boys two punishments for their indiscretion. First, of course, they were grounded for two weeks and were not allowed to watch television. Secondly, they were required to wash all of the windows at the teen residence. Mr. Hoover told them, "Maybe cleaning the windows will help to clean your minds as well." I felt bad for the guys having to wash all those windows. The building was two stories, with an attic. A lot of work for a couple of young boys.

By chance, my chore that week was policing the grounds surrounding the Harrison House. While cleaning up trash by the fire escape, I found the part of the latch that had fallen from the window. At first I didn't realize what it was. I was going to just throw it in the trash, but then remembered hearing some kind of rumor about a "peeping Tom" this past week. It was probably just a story the girls made up to get a little attention, I thought, but my sister, Mary Lou, told me that she knew for a fact that there was an "incident" and that the broken latch probably came from that window to the girls' dorm.

I put the piece of metal in my pocket. I later transferred it to my strongbox. It will serve as a reminder to me that there are probably better ways to learn about girls than being a "Peeping Tom" (or Tim)."

Chapter 14

REVENGE

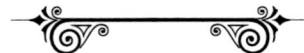

M r. & Mrs. Hunt were house parents for a while for the teenagers. Mrs. Hunt was very nice. She seemed to take an interest in the girls. She counseled them about how to dress and behave and would listen to their thoughts when they needed to talk. Ed, however, was not as nice. He was always grouchy and kind of short-tempered. He didn't seem to like having anything to do with the girls. He liked sports and liked to spend time rough-housing with the boys. But when it came time for meting out punishments, especially for the girls, he seemed to relish the idea.

One of the girls, Pat, had snuck out one evening to be with her boyfriend, Bill. She had been found out and was grounded for a month. She and the other girls felt the punishment was over the top. They wanted to get back at the jerk.

It was winter, mid-January. The day was cold, the sky was dark and the air was full of dampness. The temperature was to drop further that night. The girls were in Pat's room trying to think of a way to "teach this guy a lesson," without getting caught, of course. After much discussion, Jann came up with what they thought was a good idea. Her boyfriend, Ray, had an older car and it seemed every time they were out, the car had broken down. She remembered one time when the battery had died what a hassle the whole event had turned out to be. She said, "Let's take the battery out of Hunt's car." The girls exchanged glances. Pat said, "Good one." They all agreed that would be a great way to get back at him.

Mr. & Mrs. Hunt had to go to a short staff meeting that Tuesday afternoon, at the main building, where the administrative offices were housed. They were to be gone for about an hour. There weren't too many kids around that late afternoon because of some school activity, so Mrs. Hunt told the girls, "You are on your own for a little while. I think I can trust you girls to behave yourself." The girls assured her that she could count on them.

As soon as the Hunts were out of sight, the girls went to work. Pat was the "lookout," making sure the house parents did not return too soon. Penny popped the hood. Jann removed the battery cables, as she had seen Ray do this before. Midge lifted out the battery. Midge and Jann carried the battery down to the old "Todd Barn" as it was called. The barn had at once been used for horses when it was part of Todd School for Boys. Now the barn was used mainly for a place for teens to make out and smoke cigarettes.

The other girls were not aware of this, but Pat had also snapped off the hood ornament on the car and put it in her pocket. After all, it was Pat who had received the month's grounding. She really was upset about that. She was more angry than the other girls.

When they reached the barn, Pat, who was quite small, attempted to slide back the old wooden door. It moved slowly along its track and was heavy. Penny helped push and they got it open. There was an old horse saddle that had been abandoned years ago sitting just inside the door. The girls were able to maneuver the battery behind it. It was well hidden.

The girls rushed back to the dorm. They went to their respective rooms, just in the nick of time. Pat and Jann roomed together and Midge and Penny shared a room. They got out books from school and pretended to be doing homework. They wanted to impress the house parents with their good behavior and quiet demeanor. The house parents returned shortly. They had been gone less than an hour. Mrs. Hunt checked on the girls and said, "I knew I could count on you."

The morning bell always went off at 6:30. Everyone had a half hour to get up, take care of personal grooming, make their bed, get dressed for school and then get to breakfast downstairs in the dining room at 7:00. This morning turned out a little differently. Midge was awakened by the sound of a crashing noise about 6:00. It sounded like metal on metal. Then she heard Mr. Hunt ranting and raving. She couldn't make out all he was saying, except she was pretty sure she heard the word, "battery." Midge awoke Penny and told her to go get Pat and Jann.

By now, most of the teens had been awakened by the commotion. Mr. Hunt was at the bottom of the stairs leading to the girl's dorm and yelling, "Everybody up, right now! I want everyone downstairs immediately!" He actually ran up the stairs to the boy's dorm, entered each room and told the boys to get downstairs.

Everyone gathered in the dining room. Mr. Hunt was livid. His face was red and he looked as though the top of his head might blow off. He said, "The battery is missing from my car. I am calling the police. If any of you had anything to do with this, I am going to let you sit in jail. It is 6:45. By

7:00, I want to know who the perpetrators are. I don't think this was done by anyone else–it was one of you, I know it." Everyone was dismissed to their dorms and warned that there would be no breakfast this morning unless this mystery was cleared up.

Pat, Midge, Jann and Penny met in Pat and Jann's room. Midge said, "We'd better admit to this or everyone is going to be punished. Maybe Hunt will cool off after we tell him it was just a joke." "Cool off" and "Mr. Hunt" were probably not words to be used in the same sentence. He had a temper; all the teens knew that. The girls didn't want all the other teens to suffer and also didn't want them all to be mad, so they decided to tell Mr. Hunt the truth.

The girls went to the house parent's living room, where Mr. & Mrs. Hunt were sitting. Mrs. Hunt seemed quite calm. Mr. was still seething. Pat had decided to be the spokesperson. She was a good girl, seldom caused problems, except for that one night with Bill. She explained that she and the other girls were upset over what they felt was a harsh punishment. They thought it would be funny to play a joke on Mr. Hunt. Unfortunately, they were not aware of just how cold it was going to get that night and also didn't realize that Mr. Hunt had a class to attend the next morning at Northern Illinois University in DeKalb. Now they were really going to get it!

Mr. Hunt made the girls go to the barn, dressed as they were, with no coats, to retrieve the battery. Somehow, maybe because of the ice and snow on the hood of the car, Mr. Hunt didn't notice the missing hood ornament. To my knowledge, the issue of the hood ornament never did surface. Maybe Mr. Hunt never noticed it or thought that some student at NIU had taken it.

Mr. Hunt still wanted to call the police. The girls couldn't believe how angry he was over this silly little prank. Mrs. Hunt finally stood up and said, "I think we can move on now. The girls know they were wrong. They will be punished, but I don't think we need to involve the police." Mrs. Hunt–always the voice of reason in the relationship. Mr. Hunt finally calmed down a little and said, "Okay, I won't call the police, but it's only because I don't want more embarrassment for the home. You girls are just lucky that my wife is so good natured." The girls were sure relieved about that.

Their relief was short-lived, however, because now the punishment was coming. All four girls were grounded for a month. Mr. Hunt warned them, "And I do not expect any additional recriminations because of this harsh punishment."

He looked directly at Pat when he said this. The girls were also required to write a letter of apology to Mr. Hunt's NIU professor explaining why Mr. Hunt had missed his class that day. After Mr. Hunt left the room, Mrs. Hunt told the girls that she was, "really disappointed" that they had deceived her about their activities while she and her husband were at the main building. She then kind of chuckled and said, "Wow, that husband of mine can really blow a gasket."

Pat and I were good friends. We still are. Even dated for a while. That evening she told me all that had transpired. Even told me about the hood ornament, but swore me to secrecy. She handed me the hood ornament and asked me to dispose of it. I was reluctant at first. I certainly didn't want to get involved in this caper. But then I remembered that I had just the place to "dispose" of it.

I "disposed" of it in my strongbox. Each time I see it I think of the clever prank the girls pulled on Mr. Hunt. But it also reminds me to think before acting out in revenge.

Chapter 15

THE "MOUSE WHISPERER"

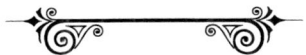

B ruce was one of the more colorful kids I remember from
the home. A bit odd. He liked mice, of which there were
always plenty in those old buildings. Not only the little
brownish gray kind of cute rodents, but also rats–I think
they refer to them as Norway rats. They were large, black,
pointy-eared and had long thick tails. Really scary looking.
You would always see them in the basement storage area. You
could hear the rodents scurrying around in the attic at night.
No one liked that sound. Once in a while a mouse or rat would
die in the walls. That left a terrible smell for a while.

Bruce had a Lionel train set in the basement of the main
building. His dad had given it to him when his dad left Bruce's
mom. It was set up on a platform of plywood. He spent a lot
of time with it and we were all jealous of it. The set had a

transformer that ran it. The transformer had two poles, I guess one positive and one negative, that when connected, would give off the electrical charge needed to power the train. One time Bruce had caught a frog and connected the legs to the transformer and electrocuted the frog. Kind of cruel and gruesome, but we boys had to act like we thought it was funny. I did not. I have always been an animal lover.

Edgar was really upset by what Bruce had done to the frog. He went to the houseparent, Mr. Knight, and told him what had happened. Mr. Knight confronted Bruce. Bruce knew better than to lie–several boys had witnessed the act. Mr. Knight gave Bruce a stern talking-to about why it was wrong to be cruel to animals and told him that his train set was "off limits" for two weeks. Bruce was pretty upset with Edgar.

We called Edgar a "square." I guess today he would be called a "nerd." He wore kind of thick glasses for such a young kid, always wore the top button of his shirt buttoned up and carried a pen protector in his shirt pocket. He was studious and quiet, but did not bother anyone else and was always polite, though rather shy.

Bruce had this ability to catch mice. Sometimes, if still alive, he would play with them. We were all a bit turned off by this, but we were glad that he was at least getting rid of some of them.

He kept a supply of mousetraps in his foot locker. Everyone knows that mice like cheese and peanut butter, but Bruce also knew that they liked natural sugars, so he would sometimes use a slice of apple to catch them. But what mice really like is chocolate. We later found out that Bruce's dad had worked for a local pest exterminator and that's how he obtained this knowledge.

Bruce wanted to get back at Edgar. He decided to use his "mouse whispering" skills. He caught a mouse in one of his traps, using chocolate. The trap snapped at just the right time and caught the neck of the mouse, killing it instantly. When Bruce found the trap, he removed the mouse and put it under Edgar's pillow.

Just after the evening's devotions and just before lights out, there was a scream. It was Edgar. He was preparing his bed for the night. He had picked up his pillow to arrange it comfortably and felt something kind of furry under it. It was a dead mouse! He immediately ran to Mr. Knight and told him about it. Mr. Knight, knowing Bruce's fondness for mice, asked him if he wouldn't mind removing it from Edgar's bed. Bruce did so, but not before terrorizing Edgar with it by rubbing it along his arm and swinging it, by its tail, in front of Edgar's terrified face. Bruce said to Edgar, "Maybe this will teach you not to be a squealer."

Mr. Knight asked Bruce if he had planted the mouse under the pillow. Bruce responded, "Yeah, I did it and I'm glad of it. That's what happens to squealers."

Mr. Knight was one of the house parents that always was able to pick just the right punishment. Some house parents would send you to bed early or make you skip dinner or just ground you, no matter what you had done. Mr. Knight was always more creative.

He said to Bruce, "Since you seem to like these creatures so well, I am going to let you spend some time with them. You are going to restack all of the canned goods in the basement. I don't care how long it takes you. You and your 'friends' can spend some quality time together." There was a lot of shelving down there with a lot of canned goods. Every time we had to go down there we would see critters. It took Bruce about three weeks to get that job done. For some reason after that, he just didn't seem to have as much interest in his mouse hobby.

I was always afraid of mice and rats. Still am. I would never have kept a mouse trap that had been used, but I did pilfer one of the new ones from Bruce's foot locker. I tucked it away safely in my strongbox. Maybe it would keep mice from trying to get into it. It would also remind me not to "squeal."

Chapter 16

"CITY SLICKER"

Larry and Eddie were brothers. Their parents lived on a farm in Sycamore, Illinois. The small town was west of Woodstock, about an hour's ride away. The father was quite a drinker and did not support the family very well. That is why the two boys had been brought to the home. The parents visited frequently and the boys occasionally went home for visits.

Steve was from Chicago. He always wanted to visit a farm. He was constantly bugging Larry and Eddie to invite him to go along one weekend when they went home so he could see what living on a farm was really like. He couldn't quite imagine how quiet it would be or what it would be like to have all those live animals around. The city was so noisy and the animals he saw were rats, feral cats and wild dogs.

Steve liked pictures he saw of corn and wheat fields and all those big machines like tractors and combines that were used on a farm.

Larry and Eddie finally relented. They liked Steve, and besides, they figured they could have a little fun with this "city slicker." The home granted permission for Steve to go to Sycamore with the boys for a weekend visit. Larry and Eddie's parents were glad to have Steve come along. It would help keep the boys occupied.

And "keep them occupied" was what it did. The first thing they did was to introduce Steve to the cows. Steve didn't know the difference between a cow, heifer or bull. Larry pointed out a large, black animal that was kind of standing by itself, a little away from the others. Larry said, "Why don't you go pet that one? It's real friendly." Steve cautiously began to approach the animal. He had never seen such a large animal, except the time that he had been to the Brookfield Zoo, but those animals were behind fences. Unknown to Steve, this animal was not just a friendly cow, as he had thought. It turned out that it was the bull. Bulls are all about self-preservation. The bull began snorting when Steve began his approach. Then he lowered his head and started pawing at the ground. Steve froze. At this time, they boys' dad had come around the barn, saw Steve in the pasture, and yelled, "You boys get the heck out of there!" Steve slowly backed up, never taking his eyes off the animal. In the process, one of his feet landed on a large, soft cow pie. Not only was he scared to death, but now his shoe was covered in cow manure. He got close to the fence, turned around and scaled it in one leap. Larry and Eddie got a huge laugh out of this. Their dad just shook his head and snickered.

The boys said, "Come on, we'll show you around the rest of the farm." They came to another area where there were more cows. Very docile animals. These were not surrounded by a fence. There was just a wire running around the area where they stood. Eddie said, "We need to cut through here to get down to the creek. Just lift that wire, Steve, and we'll go under it." Steve grabbed the wire to lift it. "ZZZtt." He felt the electrical shock go through his hand and up his arm. Not enough of a shock to cause harm, but it did hurt nonetheless. Eddie said, "Haven't you ever heard of an electric fence, city slicker?" The pain had by now subsided and Steve tried to laugh good naturedly.

The boys then went down to the creek, caught a grass snake and a frog and just wasted some time before dinner. They heard the dinner bell ring and their mom yelled, "You boys come to the house. Dinner is ready." All three boys were hungry. They had had a full day. Steve had really enjoyed being in the fresh air.

They all took places at the table. "Wow, what a spread," Steve said to himself. Mashed potatoes, gravy, sweet corn ("grown right on the farm," their dad had said), roast beef and something else Steven didn't recognize, but he thought it must be good. Everything looked delicious and there seemed to be so much food. They discussed the events of the day. Steve told them he was learning a lot about "life on the farm." They enjoyed dinner, although Steve still wondered what that one thing was.

Before they were offered that delicious looking cherry pie that was cooling on the oven top, the dad asked Steve, "So, how did you like the pig's feet?" Steve almost lost what he had eaten. Pig's feet, he thought. I just ate pig's feet? He had seen the pigs in the pen, wallowing in their own feces. He felt kind of sick to his stomach. The mom then offered pie.

Steve said, "You know, I am pretty full right now. Maybe later."

Shortly after dinner, they all went to bed. Steve didn't get sick, but he made up his mind that at future meals he would ask the name of any foods he didn't recognize. They all slept well after their full day.

Early in the morning, Steve heard the rooster. "Huh, I guess that really does happens on a farm," he thought to himself. He had thought that was just a fairy tale from his childhood. It was shortly after 5:00. Eddie told Steve, "We get up early on the farm."

The mom called the boys for breakfast. Steve's stomach was feeling better. They had a huge breakfast of scrambled eggs, sausage, fried potatoes, biscuits and freshly squeezed orange juice. Wow, too bad we don't have these kinds of breakfasts at the home, Steve thought. He was tired of hot and cold cereal most every day. And never fresh orange juice. The home came up with some strange juices, even had sauerkraut juice once in a while.

After breakfast the boys decided they would show Steve the barn. It seemed huge. There was an area of the bottom floor where a tractor, plow and some farm equipment that Steve couldn't name was stored. Beyond that, through two sliding wooden doors, were where the cows came to be milked. The father explained that they had to be milked twice a day, "come hell or high water." He told Steve that if you had milk cows, you never got a day off.

115

Larry pointed out a ladder that was attached to the wall that led to a small opening in the ceiling, just big enough for a grown man to fit through. He said, "That leads up to the hay mow. We've had a lot of fun up there over the years. I even got my first kiss up there." This intrigued Steve.

Steve said, "I want to see it." They climbed the ladder and pulled themselves onto the floor of the hay mow. Steve couldn't believe how much hay was stored up there, but it sure was dry and dusty. Immediately, he started sneezing. Larry explained to Steve that you had to carry bales of hay across the floor and toss them down to the cows below. Steve said, "Can I carry one over and throw it down?" Larry said that would be fine, but warned him that the bales were heavy and he "might get dirty."

Steve said, "Not a problem. I'm strong enough and I don't mind getting a little dirty. I'm becoming a farm boy now." Steve picked up the bale the way Larry told him to. One hand on one piece of twine and the other hand on the other string of twine. Hold the bale against your legs and just carry it over.

The bale was heavier than Steve expected, but he wasn't going to let Larry and Eddie know that. He just kept it in front of him, kind of pushing and lifting it at the same time with his legs and thighs. All of a sudden, he was falling, mid-air!

116

He landed hard, but also felt something kind of squishy. He let go of the bale and looked around. He had landed right in the middle of the cow pen in the barn. He was covered in manure. He was sure he could taste it. He heard Larry and Eddie laughing from above.

Larry said, "Now you really are a farm boy. Glad you don't mind getting a little dirty. Come on out of there and we'll hose you off."

Steve was picking himself up when he noticed something white and kind of shiny in the manure. He hated to pick it up bare handed, but he was already covered in manure. He picked it up. It looked like some sort of dog tag or something. Had a number "14" on it. He put it in his pocket. Later he noticed that all of the cows had a tag like that on their ears.

Larry and Eddy hosed Steve off and they went back to the house so Steve could put on clean clothes. Steve then said, "Hey guys, you have had your fun with me. I've been a good sport and all, but how about we call a truce? I admit that I am a city slicker." The boys agreed. They thanked him for not being angry.

Steve said, "You know, maybe someday, I can take you into the city and return the favor." Larry and Eddie were not sure they were interested.

The rest of the day was much better. Steve got to drive the tractor, saw a baby calf born, even got to shoot a shotgun. Before the day was over, Steve got to experience one more aspect of farm life.

Upon returning to the house, the boys noticed Larry and Eddie's dad doing something in the yard. Larry asked, "What's up, Dad?" His dad responded, "Just getting ready for tonight's dinner. Maybe you can give me a hand." There was a good sized white chicken running around the yard. Larry's dad instructed the boys to catch the bird and bring it to him. After a wild chase, Eddie caught the chicken and took it over to a tree stump and held it down. At that point, Eddie's dad took a hatchet out of the holder on his coveralls.

Steve asked, "What's that for?"

Eddie said, "You don't eat the head. We have to cut it off." Steve was aghast. He wondered if this was another joke. Nope, Eddie's dad skillfully, in one wave of the arm, cut off the chicken's head. Eddie removed his hands and the bird took off, running crazily around the stump for a few seconds, and then collapsed. Steve wondered if he would really be able to eat that chicken for dinner tonight.

There was a clothesline between the house and barn. Something was hanging on it, but it didn't look like clothing.

Steve asked Larry what it was, and Steve responded, "That's a rabbit. Dad shot it and skinned it. Tomorrow night's dinner." Steve was a little uneasy about this, but he was learning about how farmers really lived.

The three boys had had a fun day. They would be ready for another big dinner. While the mother was preparing dinner, the boys showered and cleaned up and then watched the early evening news, while the father finished up milking the cows.

After Larry and Eddie's dad returned from milking and showered, they sat down for dinner. The boy's dad turned to Steve and said, "What you saw out there today, the chicken and the rabbit, that's how we survive on the farm. We try to produce our own food. We take care of ourselves. Believe me, you wouldn't want to see how the meat you eat all the time is actually prepared. Hope today's farm lesson was a good one for you."

Steve looked over the table. There was a very appetizing plate of fried chicken, mashed potatoes and gravy, green beans and a nice big, fresh salad with lettuce, cucumbers, tomatoes and celery in it. And a fresh apple pie on the stove. Larry's dad said, "Steve, everything you see on this table was grown on this farm. Eat and enjoy." Steve did and he had to admit, that was the best fried chicken he had ever had.

119

After a good night's sleep, Steve was once again wakened by the rooster. Larry's dad was already milking the cows. Larry and Eddie were still sleeping. Steve slipped on his clothes and went downstairs. The boys' mom was already working on breakfast. Steve slipped out the back door, smelled the fresh air and looked over the quiet farm scene. "Beautiful, he thought, but I guess I am a city slicker at heart."

After another big breakfast (wow, these farm people sure do eat well), Larry and Eddie's parents drove them back to the home. Steve thanked them for their hospitality and their "lessons on farm life."

There was no punishment for anyone in this episode. Larry and Eddie had their fun and Steve had his weekend being a "farmer." It was a time he would always remember. I don't recall if Steve ever got the chance to "return the favor" to Larry and Eddie.

Larry and Eddie were returned to their parents not long after that. Their dad had quit drinking. I have never heard of them since. Steve was at the home for about two more years and then went back to Chicago, where he graduated from high school. I don't know what became of Steve either, but I'm pretty sure he didn't go into farming.

Before Steve left the home, he was cleaning out his foot locker. This was usually the last chore each boy did upon leaving the home. I liked being around when boys were cleaning out their foot lockers. It was always a good time to talk with each of them and many times I got some cool items they didn't want any longer. He picked up the tag with the number "14." He threw it up in the air and caught it a couple of times. "Gee, I didn't know I still had this. What a weekend that was. Hmmm, he said, after lifting the tag to his nose, still smells like manure." He tossed it in the wastebasket.

After Steve left, I retrieved number "14" and put it in my pocket. Steve was right–it still had that odor to it. Later, I put the tag in my strongbox. After hearing of Steve's experience that weekend, the tag will always remind to, "Be careful what you wish for."

Chapter 17
PISTOL

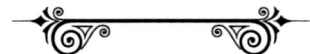

W e couldn't have pets at the home. From a practical standpoint, it just would not have worked. Literally, it would have been a "zoo." There was one occasion, however, when one of the boys had a dog for a while.

Darrell was 15 and lived at the Harrison House. He had a good friend, Mike, that lived on Grove, across the highway and about a block away. Mike's family had recently rescued a really cute dog. It was a boxer. A male, medium brown color, with a black face and ears and a nice patch of white fur on his chest. The dog had been found in an abandoned dog house on a farm with two other dogs. The other dogs had frozen to death. This one had frostbite on one ear and was seriously under weight. He had been taken to a Boxer Rescue facility in Aurora, Illinois. He was in a foster home with three other dogs. Someone had told Mike's family about the dog's plight. They went to meet him at the foster home and immediately fell in love with him. Mike, like all kids, promised that he would feed and take care of the dog.

He was a very handsome dog. Mike told Darrell that when he took the dog to the vet's office, the girl at the desk would say, "Elvis is on the floor." The girls there just loved the dog. The vet, Dr. Sepoy, really seemed to take a special interest in him as well.

The dog was very sick the first week. He could hardly keep any food down. After a couple of weeks and also a couple of hundred dollars, the dog recovered. He turned into a healthy, fun-loving dog with an abundance of energy. The vet told Mike's family that boxers tend to be "puppies" a little longer than most dogs. "Oh boy," they thought.

Mike told his dad they should name the dog, "Elvis," because of the comment from the lady at the vet's office. Mike's dad said he didn't feel that name fit him. "He is a pistol," Mike's dad said. Mike responded, "That's what we'll call him–Pistol."

Pistol turned out to be a really strong young dog. He loved to run; he was like a race horse when Mike would turn him loose in the yard. He loved people and liked other dogs. He was a "good boy." Didn't mess in the house, didn't chew up anything, almost never barked and was a joy to have around. He especially loved going over to the children's home with Mike. So many kids to play with and love! He would spend a couple of hours over there and then would be worn out for the rest of the day. He, of course, would wake up to eat. He now had a healthy appetite.

Mike told Darrell one day, while walking home from school, that his family was going to be moving away. Mike's dad worked for American Airlines and was being transferred to Tulsa, Oklahoma. Mike was not happy about it. He was going to miss his friends here, especially Darrell. Mike said the move was going to be real soon. They would be renting an apartment in Tulsa for a while. What was really upsetting to Mike was that his dad had told him they would not be able to take Pistol with them. Mike was heartbroken. He and Pistol had become such friends. He would miss him terribly.

The following Friday, again walking back from school, Mike told Darrell that the family was going to be packing tonight. He wondered if Darrell would watch Pistol over night. Darrell told Mike that he didn't think that would be allowed. But Mike convinced Darrell that the house parents were so used to Pistol being around the home that they would just assume he would be going home that night. Couldn't Darrel maybe just "hide him out" for a night? Darrell decided to do it. He really enjoyed Pistol and he also wanted to help out his friend.

As Mike had predicted, Mr. & Mrs. Everett hardly gave it a thought that Pistol was around. He was always such a joy and seemed to have a calming, almost therapeutic effect on the kids. When it was time for everyone to go to bed, Darrell just took Pistol to his room–almost as if this was what he was supposed to do. Fortunately, Darrell had the only room in the dorm that had one bed. When it was time for "lights out," Mr. Everett simply tapped on Darrel's door and said, "Good night, Darrell." Darrell responded accordingly.

The next morning Darrel snuck Pistol out to do his business, then brought him back to his room. Darrell put a couple of sausages from the breakfast table in a napkin, stuck them in his pocket and took them to his room for Pistol. Darrell knew he had to get Pistol back home. He asked Mr. Everett if it would be okay to run over to Mike's and see if they needed any help packing. Mr. Everett said that would be very thoughtful of Darrell and told him to be back by lunch time.

Pistol was put on his leash and Darrell got him down the front stairs and out the door without anyone noticing. They crossed Route 47 and headed down Grove Avenue to Mike's house. Darrell went up and rang the bell. No one answered right away. He thought they might be sleeping later, probably tired out from all that packing. He went to the back of the house to tap on the window of Mike's bedroom. When he went to knock on the window, he noticed there were no curtains. Mike's mom was probably washing and ironing them. He peeked in the window to see if Mike was in bed. Mike was not there. Neither was his bed—or any other furniture. Mike ran back to the front of the house and knocked loudly on the front door. Still no answer. Then he noticed that there were no curtains on any windows. He slid behind the landscaping and looked into the picture window. He couldn't believe what he was seeing. The house was totally empty!

He ran to check out the garage. No car. No lawnmower. No tools. Mike and his family were gone!

Darrell just stood there on the front steps for a while. He was really sad. He felt lost. There was a real pretty teenage girl that lived next door to Mike. Her name was Ruth Sherman and she was a couple of years ahead of Mike and Darrell in school. She came out on her porch and asked, "Are you looking for Mike? They left real early this morning.

You two being such good buddies, I thought you would have known that."

Darrell said, "I didn't think they were leaving so soon. They left Pistol with me."

What in the world was he going to do with Pistol? He couldn't let anyone take him to a "pound." He couldn't just turn him loose. Darrell decided then and there that he was going to keep Pistol. He got away with it for one night. Maybe, with help from other kids at the home, they could keep him and take care of him. And if he got caught, maybe just once the home would make an exception to the rules and let Pistol stay. The home really ought to have a "mascot," Darrell reasoned to himself.

Really upset, Darrel headed back to the home, with Pistol on his leash. Plans were going through his head about how he could handle this situation. Pistol needed a place to sleep, had to be fed, needed to be let out regularly. He was going to need help. Luckily, school had just let out and there would always be kids around to help with his charade. He knew the other kids would want to help him. They were all fond of Pistol.

The plan worked well for about a week. Darrell was able to get Pistol out of the building a couple of times a day for his daily routines, the other kids helped smuggle food from the table at mealtimes to feed him and since Pistol almost never barked, Darrell was able to hide him in his room. Darrell always kept his quarters very neat so Mr. Everett hardly ever came into the room.

The following Saturday morning Darrell was out real early before the other kids were up, taking Pistol for his morning walk. Apparently, Mr. Everett had gotten up early as well. He had gone down to Jeeninga's Bakery, on the square, for some donuts. As he pulled his car into the driveway, he saw Darrell and Pistol heading into the building. Darrell had not seen Mr. Everett.

Mr. Everett thought to himself, "We sure have seen a lot of Pistol lately. But where has Mike been?" He decided to investigate. He went to Darrell's room, knocked on the door and asked if Darrell would like a donut. The donut sounded good, but Darrell really didn't want Mr. Everett to come in the room. Darrell said, "Thanks, but I'm really not hungry yet." Mr. Everett said, "Darrell, I need to visit with you."

Mr. Everett entered the room and there were Darrell and Pistol sitting on the bed. Mr. Everett offered a donut once again and Darrell took it. He gave a piece to Pistol as well. Mr. Everett said, "Darrell, is there something you need to share with me?"

Tears came to Darrell's eyes. He said, "I don't want to give Pistol up. I love him." He then proceeded to tell Mr. Everett the whole story. Mr. Everett listened thoughtfully. He felt badly for Darrell. He then explained to Darrell that it just would not be possible to keep Pistol. Mr. Everett said he was fond of Pistol too, and would miss him, as would the other kids at the home.

Darrell tried his "mascot" argument. Mr. Everett said that was "very good thinking" on Darrell's part, but it would just not be practical. Darrell already knew that strategy wouldn't work, but he had given it a shot.

Mr. Everett said, "But it's not the end of the world. I know of a lady here in town who rescues boxers. I will call her." Mr. Everett called Mrs. Anderson that day. It turns out that the Andersons had recently lost one of their rescue boxers and were looking for another. Mrs. Anderson suggested they bring Pistol over for a "meet and greet" that afternoon.

Mr. Everett and Darrell took Pistol to the Andersons late that afternoon. Pistol and the Andersons immediately hit it off. There were two older female boxers at the house, and after the brief introductions and normal "checking each other out" by the dogs, they all seemed to be good with each other. Mrs. Anderson removed Pistol's collar, gave it to Darrell, and said, "We always start them out with a new collar and leash. We think it makes them feel special." Darrell was happy that Pistol had a new home. It seemed like a special home for dogs. He was also happy that Mrs. Anderson said he could visit Pistol as often as he liked.

But Darrell also knew there were going to be consequences for what he had done.

On the way home from delivering Pistol, Mr. Everett said to Darrell. "I understand why you did what you did. You have a good heart. But you know that I have to punish you, right?" Darrell nodded his head in agreement.

Mr. Everett said he had contacted the county animal shelter out on Banford Road, and asked if they needed help. The lady at the desk said, "We always need help." Mr. Everett arranged for Darrell to work, for free, for four Saturday mornings at the shelter doing whatever they asked of him. Darrell felt that was reasonable. Who knows, maybe he would find another dog for Mrs. Anderson (or even himself).

Pistol loved his new home. He was treated very well. "Spoiled rotten" is probably the better term. Ate three times a day, got treats every time he went outside, always had playmates and even had his own bed. All the dogs had their own beds, but they usually preferred curling up with one another.

Over the years, Pistol had several "sisters." The Andersons usually only took in females, and always older ones. Pistol was an exception. They thought by getting a younger dog, they might have one that would be in their lives longer. Over the years Pistol had several sisters. Their names were Maya, Rosie, Lulu, Dolly, Maxine, Curly and Samantha. As expected, Pistol outlived them all.

One day, a few weeks after Mike's family had left Woodstock, Darrell got a letter in the mail. It was from Mike. They were now settled in Tulsa. Dad's job was great. They were happy, but he sure missed Pistol. Mike apologized in the letter for leaving Pistol with Darrell the way he had, but he felt he had no choice. He was afraid that Pistol was going to end up in the pound. Mike knew that somehow Darrell would see to it that Pistol was taken care of. Mike also felt sure that the children's home would see that Pistol got a good home. The fine way that they took care of so many children over the years, how could they not do the same for a dog? Mike asked Darrell to write back and tell him what had happened with Pistol. Darrell wrote Mike back a few days later and told him of Pistol's good fortune.

Darrell had gone back to live with his parents about a year after Mike moved away. He thought about asking Mrs.

Anderson if he could take Pistol with him, but felt that would be unfair. Pistol was so happy with his sisters and new home. He decided he would get another dog.

I sat with Darrell in his room as he was preparing to leave. We talked about Pistol. He handed the leash to me and said, "I know you like dogs and were really fond of Pistol. Thanks for helping me "stash" him for a week. I want you to have this collar. You never know when another dog may come around here needing a home."

I took the collar. It had an expired rabies tag on it, along with a little silver heart with Pistol's name and Mike's parent's phone number. I put the collar in my strongbox. Every time I saw it, I thought of Pistol, Mike & Darrell. What a friendship! When I looked at it, I knew in my heart that I would always have a dog of my own. I also thought of how much I missed my friend.

Chapter 18

THE DETOUR

There was, and still is, an organization based in Wheaton, Illinois, called "Youth for Christ." The organization went by the acronym, "YFC." They had a chapter in Woodstock, which met at the children's home. The home encouraged the teens to be involved, but it was not required. Obviously it was a faith based group. It served a good purpose. It was a way for teens to meet other Christian young people and have good clean fun in an atmosphere that didn't include their parents or a lot of adults.

One Saturday evening, YFC was showing a movie, in Wheaton, about a lounge singer (I can't remember his name), who was a drunk and finally hit a low spot in his life. He found Christ, turned his life around and became a fairly popular

Christian performer, much like George Beverly Shea of the Billy Graham Crusade.

The house parents, Mr. & Mrs. Church, encouraged us to attend. Transportation to these events was generally a problem, as Wheaton was about an hour's drive from Woodstock. A local young man, Dirk Sizemore, volunteered to drive. Dirk was a member of the church we attended. He was well-liked and had a good reputation. His older brother, Arthur, also attended the church. Arthur worked at the post office and was studying to become a minister (which he eventually did). Because of the family's close association with the home and church, Dirk was approved as "chauffer."

Dirk had this beautiful new, red 1965 mustang. We all admired it. Problem was, only three passengers could comfortably ride in it, so not everyone got to attend the movie. Judy, Karen and Rick were chosen. How convenient. Dirk had always liked Judy and Rick and Karen seemed quite close.

Dirk picked up the three teens at 6:00. They drove down Route 47, got on the toll way, heading toward Wheaton. They were having a good time–talking, laughing and enjoying the ride in the cool Mustang. As they approached the Wheaton area, Dirk said, "Let's take a detour. The new movie, *Dr. Zhivago* is playing at the Hinsdale theater. I think we might like that movie better." They had time. Hinsdale was just a few miles from Wheaton. They were all in. Sounded like fun. And how would the people at the home ever know if they attended the YFC film or not?

The three of them went to see "Dr. Zhivago." Judy, Karen and Rick had to scrounge around and pool their money to pay the admission price, but they came up with the funds needed. Dirk bought popcorn and cokes for all of them. It was a great movie. All four had enjoyed it. As expected, Dirk and Judy sat together, held hands and even kissed a little. Rick and Karen, too, were pretty chummy in the back seat on the way home.

They hustled their way back to Woodstock. They all wanted to stop at the Dairy Mart in Huntley, but they were running late and also running out of money. Dirk got them home by 11:00, as had been previously agreed. The house parents didn't want to allow much time after the movie for them to get home. They felt the teens didn't need to be out in the car with too much time on their hands. They felt that is when things sometimes got out of control.

Upon their arrival, Mr. Church said, "Welcome home, guys. Tell me about the movie."

Judy said, "It was very emotional."

Karen added, "It almost made me cry."

Rick interjected, "Boy, that guy can really sing."

Mr. Church then said, "I wonder, how did you get in without your tickets? I forgot to give them to you, so I called Clayton Bauman, the director, to tell him I forgot them. Mr. Bauman said he would leave a note at the door to let you in."

The three teens were getting an uneasy feeling about this. They exchanged worried glances. Mr. Church continued, "Mr. Bauman called about an hour ago and told me that the four of you never showed up." Mr. Bauman had been to meetings at the home and knew who the kids were and was sure they had not shown. Plus, he had purposefully been looking for them. He told Mr. Church that he was pretty sure he would have recognized them. He sure hoped they were all okay.

Karen's eyes were beginning to tear up. She reached into her purse for a Kleenex. When she pulled it out, her ticket from the Hinsdale Theater fell on the floor. Mr. Church picked it up and read it. "Well, I guess this explains things," he said accusingly. The teens again looked at each other nervously.

Judy spoke up. "Okay, so we decided to take a little detour. We went to see another movie, one which as the home requires, is approved by Parents Magazine. What's the big deal?"

"The big deal, said Mr. Church, is that you lied. And what if something had happened? We would not have known where you were. I am very disappointed in all of you. And I am sure Dirk's brother and parents will be disappointed in him as well. You know that I will have to contact them. By the way, who came up with this idea anyway?" No one answered. He sent them to bed and told them he had to do some thinking about what their punishment would be.

After breakfast the next morning, Judy, Karen and Rick were called into the office. Mr. Church again explained to the teens why what they did was wrong and how disappointed in them he was. He said, "There is going to be a Revival Meeting to be held at the church next week. There will be special services Monday through Thursday nights. The three of you will be required to attend each service. End of discussion." And, of course, they were all grounded for three weeks.

After leaving the office, Karen remarked, "I wish we would have just gone and seen the movie we were supposed to see."

Judy said, "Big deal! I don't care. What's a few more church services? We had a really good time, didn't we? I think it was worth it." They all agreed.

137

I had gone into the office right after Judy, Karen and Rick left. Mr. Church was holding the ticket to *Dr. Zhivago* in his hand. He handed it to me. He said, "Here, Andy, you like history, you ought to see this movie. And it's a good love story too (not sure why he threw that remark in). I don't like what those three pulled, but it would probably be a good movie for all of us to see."

I probably should have given the ticket to Karen so she could put it in one of those plastic holders in her wallet, the way teen girls used to do. But no, I kept it and eventually put it in my strongbox. When I would see it later, it would remind me to think twice before taking "detours" in my life. As always, there are consequences.

Chapter 19

"BAD" BOYS

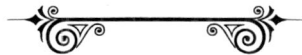

There weren't many kids at the home that I would call "bad." Most of them had been through difficult circumstances by the time they got to the home. A lot of them had trouble adjusting to the structured life, which most of them had not had. But there were two brothers who came from a local family that had a long history of being trouble makers. Glenn and Trey came from that family. I would label them as "bad."

The Free Methodist Church ran the children's home and also operated the "Old People's Rest Home," located on the next block on Route 47. At some point, the name of the home was changed to "Sunset Manor." A much better moniker. It was a good home for seniors, just as the children's home was a good home for children.

One summer day, Glenn and Trey were required to go to Sunset Manor and help the janitor there to clean and wax the tile floors in the hallways. I don't recall the incident, but they were being punished for some infraction of the rules. They were very angry about this. They didn't like old people and they didn't like work. After spending several hours helping the janitor, Mr. Robertson, clean and wax the floors, they had built up a real head of steam. They decided to exact a little revenge.

There were some residents in the lounge area watching television. The lounge area was nicely decorated, sunny and comfortable. There was a corridor off the lounge that led to the nursing station and "The Ward." The ward was where the really sick older people were sent. We all hated going in there. It was very depressing and smelled badly, of sickness, medicine and urine.

As the boys were exiting the building through the lounge area, they each grabbed a resident's wheel chair and pushed it down the hall, very quickly, scaring the occupants of the wheel chairs. They then grabbed two more and did the same. Fortunately, all of the chairs were stopped by bumping into walls. No one was hurt, but the seniors were visibly shaken.

The boys then went from room to room in the corridor and rearranged medicine bottles located on nightstands in the people's rooms. They turned pictures upside down. Then when leaving the rooms, they locked the doors so the seniors could not get back in their rooms. Finally, on their way out of the building, Glenn pulled the fire alarm and set it off. The loud, piercing noise again frightened the residents, putting them all into a frenzy.

What had these guys been thinking? It would be obvious who the culprits of this caper were. The nurse on duty, Mrs. Joosten, knew the boys were there that day. Plus she knew their names anyway from church and from when the kids at the home were sent to the manor to receive shots and vaccinations. But that was the kind of bad boys these guys were. They were the kind that didn't care if they were caught. Punishment didn't scare them. They were just interested in being mean and causing trouble.

Sure enough, they were barely back to the teen dorm when a call came from Mrs. Joosten for Mr. Brown. Mr. Brown was livid. He hunted down the boys, grabbed them by the backs of their necks and took them into the office, roughly pushing them down into chairs. Mr. Brown had at one time worked as a prison guard in another state. He had no tolerance for boys like these. He knew their kind and knew what kind of adults they would most likely become.

He said to the boys, "That was a mean, despicable and dangerous thing you did today at the manor. What do you have to say for yourselves?"

Glenn just kind of shrugged his shoulders and defiantly said, "So what?"

Trey asked, "What's the big deal? No one got hurt." Neither boy felt remorse. They just stared blankly at Mr. Brown, awaiting their punishment.

Mr. Brown told the boys that what he would "like" to do was to give them a real good beating, that maybe that is a punishment they could relate to. Mr. Brown knew that would not be allowed. He thought to himself, "Too bad we don't have solitary confinement here. That's what these 'tough guys' need."

Instead, the boys were made to run the dishwasher at Sunset Manor for a week, all three meals a day. This doesn't sound so bad, but the dishes were disgusting. The boys knew they could survive that though. The really bad part of the punishment, however, was that the boys also had to eat with the residents, three meals a day for that week. They would be required to rotate tables and get a chance to meet all of the residents.

The boys were sent to their rooms that night without dinner. That was okay with the boys. Their appetites were not very good, thinking about what they would be eating next week and who they would be eating with.

The boys hated their punishment. They had never liked or understood old people. They smelled bad, couldn't hear well, couldn't see well and gummed their food. After the first couple of days they just became numb to their feelings and decided they would just have to live with the fate bestowed upon them. Funny, but some of the residents actually enjoyed their company. It was refreshing for the seniors to have some young people around, even though these boys were not all that pleasant.

One of the old ladies had even given the boys a couple of old German coins that her late husband had saved over the years. They weren't worth anything she told them, but "I just wanted to give you something for being so kind to join us for meals." Glenn and Trey nearly choked on their food. They couldn't believe this old lady actually thought the boys were doing this out of the goodness of their hearts.

That week was the longest week of Glenn's and Trey's lives to this point. They didn't learn from the experience though. They continued to cause trouble. It wasn't too much longer before the boys were removed from the home. I know they weren't returned to their parents. Glenn died in a car accident while still a teen. Trey's life turned out badly. He got involved with booze and drugs and never amounted to much.

Before the brothers were sent away from the home, I had the opportunity to play a game of poker with Glenn, Trey and two other boys. Of course, card playing at the home was strictly forbidden. Not surprisingly, Glenn had a pack of cards. This is the only time in my life I ever played poker. I didn't even know what I was doing. I ended up winning a hand and instead of putting in a nickel, Glenn had put in the pot one of the German coins the old lady had given him. He figured it wasn't worth anything.

I was glad to get it. I put the coin in my strongbox. Whenever I see it, I think about the "bad boys." It also made me think about how wrong it was the way they treated those older people. I vowed to myself to have more respect for older people and to treat them kindly.

Chapter 20

WINSTONS

B lake, Jim and Bob were in the old chicken coop located on the main building property. Blake had a pack of cigarettes. This was not unusual. Blake was 16. He had started smoking when he was 13. His dad had let him smoke, "as long as you can pay for your own. Don't go mooching off me," his dad had told him. Jim and Bob had never smoked a cigarette, they just wanted to try it and also to impress Blake that they were cool too.

Blake tore off the rapper from the pack of Winston cigarettes, tapped the pack against his left hand and took three out. He handed one each to Jim and Bob. He put one in his own mouth, struck a match and lit it. "Hmm, he said, Winston tastes good, like a cigarette should." They were all familiar with the commercial that was currently running on TV, just before cigarette advertising was banned on television.

Jim and Bob lit up also. They immediately started coughing. Blake told them to just take their time, get used to the smoke. He was going to teach them to inhale, "like a man." The smoke was filling the room, even though it was not enclosed.

Next door, Mr. Gardner, the maintenance man, was puttering in the work shed, probably getting ready to mow the yard with that small tractor with the mower attached behind it. Bob always wanted to use that, but the home said you had to be at least 16 years old.

Mr. Gardner smelled smoke. He came out of the shed, looking around. He could see smoke wafting out of the chicken coop. He was alarmed and hurriedly ran into the coop. There he saw the three boys, all with cigarettes in their hands. The boys immediately dropped them and crushed them out on the cement floor.

"Hey, Mr. Gardner yelled, you guys are not supposed to be smoking. Where did you get the cigarettes? Did you steal them? I suppose it was you that started this, Blake. You're always an instigator!" Well, if you want to smoke, you are

146

going to get this out of your system today. You'll never want to smoke again."

Mr. Gardner made the boys smoke the whole pack, one after another, until their faces turned a greenish pallor and they all threw up. Their throats hurt from the wretching. Their eyes were sore from the smoke. Mr. Gardner made them stay and clean up the mess they had made. Then they had to hose down the chicken coop.

Mr. Gardner said, "I should report this to your house parents, but I think you may have learned your lesson. Smoking is bad for you. You can see now how sick it can make you Oh, and tell me, does Winston tastes good, like a cigarette should?" He laughed at his own joke. He was familiar with the commercial too.

Mr. Gardner sent the boys on their way. He told them if he ever caught them smoking again, he "would not let them off so easy." The three teens went back to their respective rooms after that. They still felt sick and they were worried that despite what he had said, that Mr. Gardner might still tell their house parents what had happened and then they would be punished again.

Mr. Gardner should have retrieved the empty cigarette pack and matches and disposed of them, but I think he was having too much fun watching the boys wretch, and forgot about them. When they returned to the dorm, I had passed them on the stairs. Blake reached into his pocket, where one cigarette remained in the pack and tossed the pack to me and said, "Here, want a smoke?" I didn't know why he did that. Blake was always a little unpredictable.

I just accepted the pack and said, "Thanks," and walked to my room. I didn't smoke at that time. I just threw the package with one cigarette in my nightstand drawer. Maybe I would try it some time later.

The next day word had gotten around the dorm about what had happened in the chicken coop. Blake had told Jim and Bob to "keep their mouths shut about it," but Jim told his roommate (sworn to secrecy, of course) and the word got out. As far as I know, the house parents never found out.

After hearing the story, I decided to put the cigarette pack, with the one cigarette, in my strongbox. It would remind me of how sick the boys got and would hopefully prevent me from taking up the habit. (That didn't work–I eventually took up the habit myself). I don't smoke Winstons, though–Blake later told me that "they taste bad."

Chapter 21

"NOT GUILTY"

M r. & Mrs. Wisner were good house parents. They seemed to care about the kids. They were generally fair and objective and had the best interests of the kids at heart. There was one incident, however, where Mr. Wisner acted out of character.

Mr. Wisner was somewhat of a history buff. Part of the reason, I guess, was that his great-grandfather had served in the Spanish-American War in 1898. He had fought in Cuba, not along side Teddy Roosevelt, but at the same time and in the same area. Mr. Wisner's great-grandfather had given Mr. Wisner a fancy belt buckle that he had worn during the war. It was over-sized, silver, with a horse's head emblem on it, much like a cowboy would wear. It also had a dent in it. The dent was supposedly from a bullet fired by a Spanish soldier. Mr. Wisner had told the kids, "the buckle saved my great-grandfather's life. Mr. Wisner had been given the belt buckle when he was a boy of eight. The buckle was the most precious thing he owned.

One Saturday morning Mr. Wisner noticed the buckle was not in its usual spot on his dresser. He asked his wife about it and she indicated that she had not moved it and didn't recall seeing it recently. "Could you have misplaced it?" she asked.

He said, "No way. I always leave it in the same spot." Mr. Wisner was dumbfounded and was very quickly becoming angry. He shouted, "I'll bet one of these kids stole it. Someone's going to pay for this." He stormed out of the room.

Mr. Wisner gathered all of the kids together. He didn't mince his words. He told them of the missing buckle. He said that he was pretty sure that one of them had taken it. He made it clear to them how much the buckle meant to him. "Here's the deal, he said. I want that back in the worst way. Whoever has it, just return it. I will accept it with no questions asked. No one will be punished. I will even offer a reward. Whoever brings me back the buckle will receive either $20.00 cash or this nice pocket knife that has never been used." The pocket knife was still in its original packaging. It wasn't real big, but very nice looking. He reiterated that no questions would be asked and no one would be punished. He just had to have that belt buckle back. "It is 9:00 Saturday morning. You have until 5:00 tomorrow night to return it. After that, all bets are off. Someone, or maybe all of you, will be held responsible if it is not returned."

Five o'clock Sunday came and went. No one brought the belt buckle to Mr. Wisner. He was still stewing mad. He didn't say anything to anyone. He had already decided that on Monday, while the kids were in school, that he was going to go through each boy's and girl's rooms and do a thorough search. The treasured belt buckle was probably still in the building. He sure hoped no one had taken it and then sold it or given it away.

As planned, right after everyone left for school on Monday morning, Mr. Wisner began his search. Mrs. Wisner, reluctantly, worked on the girls' side of dorm, while Mr. Wisner concentrated on the boys' side. It was unusual for a search like this to be conducted. Usually, a notice was given ahead of time that there would be an inspection of rooms, presumably to make sure everyone was keeping things in order.

The belt buckle was not found despite Mr. & Mrs. Wisner's best efforts. Some other interesting items were found though. An unopened pack of condoms was found in one boy's dresser, one cigarette and a pack of matches was found in one girl's nightstand. One girl had a pretty trashy paperback book in a drawer. Some bullets were found in one of the boy's room. No gun, of course, but where had the bullets come from?

Wednesday was Veteran's Day and the kids had a day off from school. Mr. Wisner announced at breakfast that this morning there was going to be a "work period" for an hour. Everyone was to prepare their rooms for an "inspection" to be done later in the morning. He didn't tell them that he was aware that some of the kids had items they should not have. He didn't want them to know that he had gone through their things. He even indicated that he and his wife would be doing the same thing to their apartment, attempting to put on an air of innocence about the whole episode.

I always kept a neat, clean room. The only contraband I had was in my strong box. It didn't take me long to get my room in order. After I was done in my room, I went to Mr. & Mrs. Wisner and asked if they needed any help. They gladly accepted my offer. Mr. Wisner asked me to help him move their bedroom dresser. He said, "I see dust bunnies behind it." We moved the dresser out from the wall and then I ran the dust mop behind and under it. The dust mop caught on something. I got down flat on my belly and reached under the dresser. It was some kind of square, burgundy colored, velvet-covered case. I handed it to Mr. Wisner and said, "This was under the dresser."

Mr. Wisner exclaimed, "Oh my God, I don't believe this.' He sat on the edge of his bed and tears actually came to his eyes. He said, "Oh, Andy, this is the belt buckle. I thought it was gone for good. I can't believe you found it."

The box had apparently fallen off the dresser and had become wedged perfectly in the dark corner where the back and side of the dresser fit together. Mr. Wisner said he had looked under the dresser, but should have moved it. Mr. Wisner hugged me and thanked me profusely. He told me that I truly was a "detective." He asked me to please not say anything to the other kids about this. Mr. Wisner needed to make the announcement himself.

After I left the room, Mr. Wisner asked Mrs. Wisner to come into the room. He showed her the buckle and explained where it had been. Mrs. Wisner was overjoyed for him, but had a look of concern on her face. She said, "Richard, you made a big mistake. How are you going to handle this with the kids?"

He said, "You are right. I am ashamed of my actions. I will take care of this."

Mr. Wisner felt terrible. He had lost his temper, had falsely accused the kids of stealing and had sneakily gone through their personal items. It was almost lunch time. He decided he would make his statement at lunch, while everyone was present. That is exactly what he did. He announced to the group, "I have some very good news to report to all of you. The belt buckle has been found." There seemed to be mixed emotions showing on the faces around the tables. No one seemed to have any knowledge of where it had been found, if someone had turned it in or exactly what this all meant.

Mr. Wisner continued, "I have an apology to make to all of you. I simply misplaced this valuable keepsake. I wrongly assumed that one of you took it. That was wrong of me. I sincerely apologize to each and everyone of you for my thinking and the way I carried on. I hope you have it in your hearts to forgive me. Their was silence and then slowly, there was the sound of clapping in the room. Everyone was relieved—relieved that the buckle had been found, relieved that there would be no group punishment and relieved that this one time they were all innocent.

Mr. Wisner explained how the buckle had been found, that Andy Moss had actually found it and therefore deserved the reward. He could have either the $20.00 or the pocket knife. The money was sure tempting, but I wanted that knife. I already had a small pocket knife, but this one was special I said, "I'll take the knife."

Mr. Wisner handed me the knife and said, "But you understand it needs to stay in your drawer."

Mr. Wisner also told the group that he felt so bad that he was calling off the inspection today. "I should be more trusting of all of you." He also told the group that he was buying "Coachlight Pizza" for everyone tonight. Pizza was a bigger treat in the early 1960's. Pizza places weren't abundant in small towns like they are now and was a treat the kids at the home rarely got.

Several of the kids indicated to Mr. Wisner that they were glad the belt buckle had been recovered. A couple of the kids felt badly that Mr. Wisner had originally doubted them. At least the ordeal was over and the Wisner's knew none of the teens had stolen the treasured buckle.

So I wouldn't be tempted to carry that beautiful knife around in my pocket, I stored it away in my strong box. This crime souvenir had special meaning. There really wasn't an actual crime, although I suppose one could argue that Mr. Wisner's original attitude might have been a bit "criminal." It was special because it would remind me that some things are worth keeping as a collectible or keepsake. It would also remind me not to be too quick to judge or accuse.

Chapter 22

"DON & TINA, SITTING IN A TREE..."

Y ou guessed it, "k-i-s-s-i-n-g" Well, not actually sitting "in"
a tree, but maybe under a tree.

The home and the house parents worked hard to discourage boy/girl relationships. It is easy to see why these
relationships at the home would be very difficult, especially
with the boy and girl living under the same roof. But as one
can imagine, some of those relationships did happen. Most
were short-lived. There were numerous sexual escapades. But
one relationship stood out.

Don came to the home from a small town in southern
Illinois. He came from a Free Methodist background. I
believe his father had passed away at a young age. Don was
a tall, skinny kid with a nice smile and ready laugh. He was
intelligent and did well in school. He never got in trouble,

but seemed to enjoy watching and viewing what others were doing. If boys were sitting around telling dirty jokes, Don wouldn't join in, but would lay on his bed laughing with the rest. He would enjoy hearing about some of the exploits of his peers, but never got into any trouble himself. Don was pretty devout about his Christianity for such a young man. The other guys on the dorm floor referred to him as, "The Chaplain."

It was interesting that Don was called that, because his girlfriend's father had actually been a chaplain in the army. Her dad was now retired from the service and taught at the local junior high. Tina's parents moved to Woodstock when she was in junior high. Her brothers were considerably older than her, "more like uncles," she once remarked. Her parents were older than most parents of her peers. I think it was for that reason that Tina was raised in the children's home.

Tina was tall, just like Don. She, too, had a nice smile. She was a shy girl and she always followed the rules as well. I think she felt that she had to behave better than anyone else because her parents went to the Free Methodist Church and her dad taught locally. She felt that she was constantly being watched and that she was expected to set a superior example to the other kids. It was like living in a fish bowl to her.

Tina was bright and talented. She was always on the honor roll, with near perfect grades. She was artistic and played the saxophone in the high school band. She had a pretty singing voice. Tina was quite a gifted writer for a girl her age as well.

Don and Tina sat across from each other in Mr. Swartout's biology class. They would steal glances at each other, thinking the other one didn't notice. Don would always take his time getting up from his seat so he would be sure to be close to Tina when she left the room. Sometimes he would follow her to her locker between classes. Tina began to notice his attentiveness. She had even noticed lately at the home that Don always seemed to be nearby.

One night at the Harrison House, after study hall, some of the kids were watching television. The other kids began going to their rooms. Tina wanted to finish watching this episode of the show she was watching. Don didn't seem that interested in the show, but remained seated. All of a sudden, they were the only two left in the room. Tina could feel Don watching her. She liked the feeling, even though it made her feel a little uneasy, in a good way. Tina decided she was going to confront Don and find out what was on his mind.

She had been doing some laundry, as the high school girls were required to do. The laundry room was just down the hall from the TV room. It was pretty private. Tina looked at Don and said, "Hey, I've got a real heavy load of clothes in the laundry room. Would you mind helping me carry it upstairs?" Don nearly jumped out of his chair, looking for a way to please her.

Tina led the way to the laundry room. When they got into the room, Tina closed the door. Don got a funny look on his face and began to blush. Tina knew right then that he liked her, but also knew that he was too shy to make a move. She walked up to him, put her arms on his shoulders, looked him in the eye and said, "I know you want to kiss me, Don. Why don't you just do it?"

Don had never kissed a girl before, but he really wanted to kiss Tina. He clumsily leaned his head down and lightly kissed her on the lips. They were both ecstatic. Don said, "You really didn't need help with the laundry, did you?"

Tina said, "No, I didn't, but I knew you needed help with me." They both giggled, smiled and kissed again. This kiss lasted a little longer and was less clumsy.

Unfortunately, they heard footsteps coming down the hall. Tina quickly opened the door. One of the other girls, Donna, with her head full of red hair, came in, cast them a kind of knowing look, and asked if Tina was done with her laundry.

Tina said she was and that Don was kind enough to help her carry the heavy basket upstairs.

On Saturday, after morning chores, Don kept hanging around the office area of the building. The office was located real close to the bottom of the staircase leading to Tina's dorm. He knew if he waited long enough, she would be coming down. If nothing else, she would have to come down for lunch. That kiss last night had really done something to Don. He just couldn't get Tina off his mind.

Finally, Tina came down the steps. Don was seated on the sofa, facing the staircase. When she appeared, Don thought she looked different. She looked prettier than ever. She seemed to have a special smile that day. Maybe that kiss had affected her the same way it did him.

Don approached her. "Good morning, Tina," he said.

She said, "Hi Don, why aren't you with your buddies?" Don told Tina that he needed to prepare better for the biology test they were having on Monday. He asked if they could study together after lunch. It was Saturday and he knew most of the kids would be out somewhere. Don had thought about this and wanted to get Tina alone again.

Tina said, coyly, like she was reading his mind, "I think I could find some time to help you out." Neither of them needed "help." They were both getting "A's" from Mr. Swartout, not an easy task. Of course, they both knew this wasn't about biology–not the kind Mr. Swartout taught anyway. They agreed to meet in the downstairs dining room at 1:00.

Don was there early. He couldn't wait. Tina, being a smart girl, thought it would be best to be just a little bit late. Make him want her more. She shuffled in about 1:10, biology text in hand, and sat down directly across from Don. Don could smell her perfume. Why hadn't he noticed that before?

They actually tried to do some studying, but it was useless. They kept looking at each other, smiling and finding excuses to touch. After a while they were even "playing footsies" under the table. Don was getting braver. He asked Tina, "Do you have any more laundry you need help with?

Tina blushed, "As a matter of fact, I do need to do some ironing." No one else was in the basement so they headed to the laundry room. This time Tina didn't need to take the initiative. They were barely inside the room and Don took her in his arms and kissed her a long time. They came up for air and kissed again.

Darn! Footsteps. It was Donna again. This time she remarked, "You guys need to find a better spot." You sure aren't fooling me. But your secret is safe with me. Actually, I'm a little jealous. You two make a nice couple."

From that point on, Don and Tina were nearly inseparable. They walked to school together. They walked home together. They would sit together at study hall. They wanted to sit together in church, but Tina's parents required her to sit with them. Tina didn't think they were aware of her relationship with Don. If they had been, they certainly would have tried to put an end to it. They didn't want her dating anyone, although they may have approved of Don, if anyone, even if he was from the home.

It wasn't long before all the kids and the house parents knew of Don & Tina's romance. The kids at that point didn't think it was a big deal. They weren't the first kids at the home to have a romance. Most of them didn't last long. The house parents certainly hoped that was going to be the case this time. It didn't work out that way though. Don and Tina really seemed to care for each other.

Don and Tina naturally had the same house parents, who talked with them and tried to discourage the relationship, at first forbidding them to "date." After a while it became a lost cause for the house parents. It was quite apparent that it was going to be very difficult for the house parents to keep them apart. They would have to just monitor the situation as best they could and provide good guidance.

Don and Tina were allowed to go to the movies together. As this was a group setting and they walked to the theater, the home felt the two of them couldn't get too involved. But Don and Tina were teenagers. They always found a way. On the way home from the show, they would stop behind Clay Street School, which was just a couple of blocks away from the home. It was quiet, dark and private. That was where they did some pretty heavy necking. Once in a while, they were able to sneak off to the Todd Barn, although it usually had to be with another couple.

The home did not allow kids to go to dances. Tina's parents did not approve of it either. So there were no sock hops, homecomings or proms to attend. They did get to go to the roller rink in McHenry, when the home went as a group. Sometimes there were church activities to attend, which allowed them to be on a "date" like other teens in attendance. They got involved with YFC so they could spend time together away from the home.

After a time, some of the other teens at the home got a little jealous of the relationship between Don and Tina. Some of these kids had boyfriends and girlfriends at school and they could not spend the time together that Tina and Don could. This created additional stress for the house parents when the other teens would voice their opinions. It sometimes caused consternation for Tina and Don as well. These kids were their friends.

After Don turned sixteen, he got a driver's license. Of course he couldn't have a car, but he did have a friend that was able to use his dad's car. Don and Tina asked for permission to go on a double date with Don's friend, Gary, and his girlfriend, Sue. This request was quickly denied. Don and Tina accepted this at first, but then realized that some of the other girls were allowed to go on dates in cars. Why should they be treated differently? At last the house parents agreed. Don and Tina had to follow the same rules as the others, which were pretty strict.

Don and Tina found that with this additional freedom also came more temptation. They became more passionate, egged on by Gary and Sue's antics. It became more and more difficult for them to control their emotions. But they did. They had made up their minds that they were going to prove the home wrong. Tina was going to save herself for marriage and Don respected that, even though it was difficult at times.

At prom time during their junior year, they were both dejected. Both would have liked to go to prom. All of their friends were going. They told the home that they would not dance. They even offered to sign an agreement stating such. And there were chaperones there that could make sure they didn't. The house parents were instructed to say, "No, we can't start making exceptions like that."

Don was in my room telling me about this. I felt bad for him and Tina both. I offered, "Don, why don't you borrow someone's car and take Tina to some fancy restaurant for dinner? Get all dressed up and have your picture taken together. Make it look like you were at the prom. You'd have that picture as a memory and you could always call it your prom night."

Don liked the idea. He took Tina to the Abby in Lake Geneva, Wisconsin. They both dressed up fancy and Tina had her hair done as if she was going to the prom. Don had bought her flowers. He even got someone at the restaurant to take a picture. It was taken in a room that was being decorated for a wedding. It really did look like a prom picture.

Don and Tina dated through high school, attended Spring Arbor College together and eventually married and had three children. The have been married over forty years! They have both been successful in the publishing world. Tina has authored several books and is an accomplished musician.

I don't recall Don and Tina ever being punished for anything. They really didn't deserve it. They were really good kids. They were truly in love after that first innocent kiss in the laundry room. I wonder if they still have clandestine meetings in their own laundry room.

Don had some extra pictures taken from their "prom night." He gave one to me and said, "Hey, thanks for helping me out. The night turned out great."

I put the photo in my strongbox. When I see it, I think fondly of Don and Tina. It made me hope that someday I would find the kind of love they had. Sadly, it also reminded me of that silly rule the home had about "no dancing."

Chapter 23

"PARTY LINE"

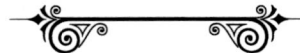

There weren't a lot of telephones around the home. The Harrison House had one in the office and there were a couple other jacks, one located in the basement dining room and one in the house parent's apartment. Phone usage was monitored closely. There were always about a dozen teens in the building and nearly everyone wanted to use the phone at some point. Long distance calls were prohibited, unless specific permission was granted. If a teen did make a long distance call, they were required to reimburse the home for the call.

Kids had to be careful on the phone. Other kids were always trying to get ahold of the only other phone in the house to attempt to listen in on conversations. The house parents would sometimes do the same. It was like being on a "party line." Like the phone my Aunt Mary and Uncle Syd had in Milford, Illinois, when I was very young. I remember the operator would come on the line and say that another call was coming in for someone else and you had to get off the phone. Grandpa was always concerned for an elderly widow that lived down the road. She was in poor health and Grandpa was worried that she wouldn't be able to get through to the doctor if someone was on the phone too long.

Of course there were phone booths back then. One was located on Main Street, by the Miller Theater and there was one on the corner next to the Opera House. But they were used a lot, weren't very clean, and you needed to have money!

Cris had been to California over the summer to visit her dad. While there, she had met a boy named David. They wrote letters to each other and David had called her a couple of times. But when he called, there was always someone else in the room and they really couldn't have a private conversation. Cris was afraid that David was going to lose interest in her. She wanted to talk with him with no one else around.

She devised a plan. She wrote him, telling him that she would call him at a specific time, adding that she, "would be alone." The time for the call was around midnight on a particular date.

On the prearranged date, Cris had taken the extra phone out of the office late in the evening. It was late enough that no one would be looking for it to call anyone. She hid it in a dining room cabinet in the basement. This was easy, as it was her turn to do dinner dishes that week, along with her roommate, Sally. Cris had told Sally of her plan, so that made everything easier to accomplish.

Cris set her alarm for 11:45 PM, although she didn't need it. She was too keyed up to sleep, thinking about the long conversation she would have with David. Just before midnight she slipped out of her room. The easy way to the basement would have been to simply walk down the stairs, which went all the way to the basement. The problem with that was that the staircase was located right over the house parent's bedroom. Not only were the stairs very creaky, but Mr. Rose was known to be a light sleeper. Instead, Cris had left the back door to the kitchen area unlocked. She hoped that no one had decided to check it later that night. Instead of taking the stairs she went down the fire escape which emptied out right by the back door to the kitchen. She was as quiet as a mouse since the fire escape was located right outside the house parent's apartment.

She got to the bottom of the fire escape, crept to the base-

ment entrance and walked down the few concrete steps. The

steps were cold on her bare feet. There were large, hard maple

leaves at the bottom of the steps. She hoped they didn't make

too much of a crunching noise when she stepped on them.

And she sure hoped there were no spiders or a snake down

there. She wished she had worn tennis shoes instead of no

shoes at all.

She reached for the door knob. She was in luck! No

one had locked it. She was afraid that if someone had, she

wouldn't be very good at getting the door unlocked with the

knife she had taken from the kitchen. She had seen George

Spencer open a door with his knife one time and figured she

could do the same if necessary.

She had to operate in the dark. Again, the darn kitchen

was located beneath the house parent's apartment and Mr. or

Mrs. Rose might see a light if they had to get up during the

night for some reason. ("Man, she thought. I can't catch a

break here. Everything is located right by the Rose's apart-

ment"). She made her way to the cabinet where she had

stowed the phone behind some large pots and pans. She very

carefully and quietly took the pots and pans off the shelf and set them on the counter, removed the phone and put the pots and pans back in the cabinet.

The phone jack was located along the floor near the refrigerator. She went into the dining area and got a chair which she carried back into the kitchen. Wow, she didn't remember these chairs being so heavy, but she got it in there without banging into anything. She set it down in front of the refrigerator and sat on the floor.

She had a small flashlight, a souvenir from Disneyland, a theme park she visited while in California. She hadn't had any use for it until tonight. The light helped her see the phone number she had written on the back of a card from her dad's dentist. She accidentally dropped the card and it landed just under the refrigerator. She would get it later. The flashlight also gave her the light she needed to dial the rotary phone without turning on an overhead light. She dialed. Boy that phone seemed to make a loud noise as that little dial kept returning after each number!

Finally, the call was going through. David answered on the second ring. "Oh good, thought Cris, he must be anxious to talk to me." She could tell by his voice that he was. It was difficult for Cris to keep her voice low. She was so excited to be speaking with David. She could tell by his voice that he was excited too. They talked about what they had both been doing since she returned from California. She indicated that her life had been pretty boring and that she missed him terribly.

David said, "I miss you too." He said he was keeping busy playing American Legion baseball. The team was doing pretty well.

They talked about the night David had borrowed a friend's car and they had gone down to the beach. They sure had steamed up the windows of the car that night! David had given her a necklace that night. It was inexpensive, a silver chain with a dolphin on it, but Cris loved it. She never took it off. It always reminded her of that night on the beach.

They talked and talked. Both were so happy. They talked about when Cris might be coming back to visit her dad. Cris said, "I hope for Christmas, if my dad can get the money together for a ticket." Cris was saving her money too. She did babysitting most weekends, but was hoping to get a better job, maybe at one of the local drive-ins or maybe at one of the lunch counters on the square, like *Woolworth's, Whipple's or Hubert's*. She had heard the girls who worked at those places made some decent tips.

Finally, David asked if maybe they should get off the phone. He didn't want her getting into trouble. She said, "Oh, we haven't been on that long." She checked her watch. "Oh, my God," she nearly shouted into the phone. "We've been talking for almost two hours. You're right, I had better go." They exchanged vows of love and hung up.

Cris retraced her steps out the door, locking it this time, back up the fire escape and to her room. She couldn't believe it. She had pulled this off. And because she had "reversed the charges," no one would ever know the call had been made. First thing in the morning, she would have to tell Sally how well everything had worked out.

Two weeks later, Cris was called into the office by Mr. & Mrs. Rose. They had an envelope and some kind of type-written column of numbers on it. One entry was circled in red ink. Mrs. Rose handed the paper to Cris, which turned out to be a phone bill. Cris's heart sank. Why was David's number showing up on the bill? She had reversed the charges. Mrs. Rose explained that even though the charges are reversed, the number still shows up and so does the length of the conversation–1 hour and 52 minutes! Mrs. Rose explained that when Mrs. Jacobson received the bill at the main office, she "went through the roof." She had contacted the phone company and found that the number was to a "David Warner" in Palisades, California. They checked and found that was her boyfriend David's number. Worse yet, the call was made at 12:03 AM.

Mr. Rose said, "Cris, we can't begin to tell you how many rules you have broken here." You are in real trouble.." Mrs. Rose went on, "We have discussed this with Mrs. Jacobson and she wants to know that you will be properly disciplined."

Cris's phone privileges were suspended for a month. If David called, he would be told that "Cris will not be available for a few weeks." If he sends a letter, we will hold on to it until that 30-day period is up."

Cris broke into tears. "You can't do this to me. David will lose interest in me and find someone else."

Mrs. Rose said, "You should have thought about that before you pulled this stunt. This is all your own fault." Cris asked if she could leave.

Mrs. Rose nodded her head, but Mr. Rose spoke up, "Oh, by the way, Cris, you are also grounded for that same 30 days."

Cris yelled, "I hate this place," and stomped out of the office, up the stairs and into her room, where she laid on her bed and cried for at least an hour.

The following Saturday, my chore was to mop the kitchen and dining room floor. As I was sweeping first, the broom pushed a business card out from under the refrigerator. I picked it up and looked at it. What was a business card doing here for a dentist in Palisades, California? I turned it over. There was a notation: "David," with a heart after it and a number. It all of a sudden hit me. Sally had told a couple of us kids about what Cris had done. I remembered that her boy-friend was from California.

I didn't give the card back to Cris. I am sure she had the number memorized. If not, I knew she could get it from the phone bill, although I doubted that she would want to ask Mr. & Mrs. Rose for it.

I put the card in my strongbox. I doubted I would ever use that dentist, and would probably have no reason to call "David," but it would remind me that no matter how careful you are, there is always a way you will be found out. It also made me a little sad for Cris. How heartbreaking young love can be.

Chapter 24
"HOME AWAY FROM HOME"

The children's home was really a pretty good place to live. Despite all the rules and no privacy, we shouldn't have complained. The house parents didn't beat us. We were warm, had clothes to wear, got three meals a day and were generally well cared for. It was funny, there were actually kids at school who would have liked to live at the home. One such teenager was a local girl named Joyce.

Joyce's home life was tough. Her mom had married young, having been pregnant at a very young age. She was now on her third husband. He was not a nice man. He beat Joyce's mom when he drank. He was always eyeing and touching Joyce and her younger sister Betty. Joyce knew it was only a matter of time before the touching would turn into something more sinister.

The stepfather seldom worked, so there was never enough money in the household. Her mom worked as a waitress and did the best she could. Joyce and Betty did whatever odd jobs they could to help out.

Joyce was a tough looking girl. She hung around with the group of kids referred to as "greasers." They wore their hair longer than most kids. They guys always had an extra button open on their shirts. The girls wore their skirts tight and short and usually dressed in mostly black clothing. The greasers hung around together in high school and liked to hang around together on the square in their free time. They were always smoking and trying to look tough.

Joyce's hair was a cheap looking bleach blond, which she wore all teased up. She dressed provocatively and had a mouth like a truck driver. She was known to get into fights with other girls. She didn't care at all about her grades and took no part in school activities. She just wanted to get out of school and get out of her home.

Joyce became friends with a couple of girls from the home, Angel and Stacey. Angel and Stacey were not greasers, but they tended to like to appear a little tougher than they were. Both girls had come from bad home situations themselves, so they understood where girls like Joyce and Betty came from. Angel and Stacey felt like Joyce did–"just get us out of here."

One morning at school, before classes started, Angel and Stacey were in the girls bathroom, just off the auditorium. Joyce came in. She looked really bad. She had a black eye, a cut lip and it was obvious that she had been crying. Angel said, "Joyce, what happened to you? Did you get into a fight?" Joyce just stared ahead.

Stacey asked, "Did your stepdad do this to you?" Joyce nodded and ducked into a stall for some privacy. Angel and Stacey could hear her sobbing.

The bell rang, indicating classes were going to begin in a few minutes. Joyce came out of the stall and said, "We need to talk later. I have to get away from that guy. I need your help." The three girls agreed to meet at lunch time. They would meet in the girl's locker room. It was free during that lunch period.

They met at about 12:15 in a back corner of the locker room. No one else was around. Joyce immediately started talking, "Can I come live with you guys at the home? I can't stay at my house any longer." Angel and Stacey looked at each other. They couldn't believe what they were hearing. Joyce actually wanted to live at the home? Things must really be bad for her. They told Joyce they were sure she would need her parent's authorization to go to the home. Joyce said, "That ain't going to happen. They would think they were airing their dirty laundry in public."

Angel told Joyce, "You are our friend. We will find a way to do this. Can you wait another night? We have to figure this out."

Joyce said, "I'll find someplace to spend tonight, but I hope you're able to help. I just have to get out of there." Then she added, "And I am so worried about Betty too."

Angel and Stacey walked home from school together, as they always did. They had a serious discussion about Joyce's situation. They decided that, one way or another, they would find a way to help Joyce out. First, they would feel out the home's social worker, Mr. Waymeer. Stacey had an appointment with him today at 4:30, for her usual monthly visit that each child was required to have. Stacey would bring Angel along and they would discuss a "hypothetical situation" with him. They would at least try to do things the right way. If that didn't work out, they would find another way to help their friend.

Mr. Waymeer, as always, was a good listener. He was young, but seemed smart for his age, and was always fair.

The girls explained their friend's situation and told him, "She would like to come live at the home."

Mr. Waymeer said, "I can understand why she would feel that way and I think it would probably be a good move for her, but these things take time. There are legal issues involved. I think you need to let her and her family work this out. You might tell her to contact a relative she can trust, or maybe a school counselor–maybe even the police."

Stacey and Angel felt depressed after leaving Mr. Waymeer's office. They had thought a direct, honest approach would work. They didn't understand. With all the kids at the home already, why would it be so difficult to help out one more? Why couldn't she just be a "visitor" for a few days? That was allowed once in a while. They were walking back to the Harrison House from the main building where Mr Waymeer's office was located, when Stacey suddenly stopped and took hold of Angel's arm. Excitedly, she said, "That's it! Joyce can be a visitor, but nobody else will know. We will let her stay in our room. This could be fun."

Angel agreed, "You're right. We can do this for a few days, until Joyce finds another place to live. And we will make it fun!"

The three friends met in the same bathroom again in the morning. Joyce looked a little better this morning, but the black eye was difficult to hide. Angel asked her, "Where did you stay last night?"

Joyce told her, "At Nancy's Milar's house. Her mom wasn't too keen on the idea though." Mrs. Milar "didn't want to get involved with someone else's problems; she had problems of her own to deal with." She allowed Joyce to stay the one night, "but that would be all."

Joyce asked, "Did you guys ask the home for me?"

Angel said, "We asked, but they gave us this 'mumbo jumbo' answer, which basically meant, "no." But don't worry, we have our own plan."

Stacey interrupted, "You are going to be our guest for a few days. We are going to hide you out until you are able to make other arrangements. It might be risky, but we will make it fun."

Joyce said, "I'm in. I even have a bag already packed."

"Good, said Angel, let's meet right here after school." They met in the bathroom after the last class of the day and walked the mile home from school together, making plans all the way. They were all a little scared, but also kind of giddy with excitement.

When they arrived at the home Angel went right to the office to "check in," as had to be done every day. Mrs. Barty asked, "Where's your sidekick?" Joyce and Stacey had quietly snuck upstairs.

Angel said that Stacey had to go to the bathroom and would be right down. Stacey came into the office and said, "I'm home." All was going well so far.

Unfortunately, the room that Angel and Stacey shared only had two single beds, but they didn't want Joyce to have to sleep on the bare floor, so they just pushed the beds together. It would be like a pajama party they thought. They had placed a chair in front of the door, with the back under the door handle. That way, if anyone were to come in, it would take a little longer, and Joyce could slip into the closet. They were so excited! For the next couple of hours, before dinner, they just talked and laughed.

When the dinner bell rang, Stacey told Joyce, "Just stay in the room. Keep the chair against the door. We will bring you dinner."

It wasn't easy sneaking food upstairs. The girls had to wait until everyone else was finished eating and then put Joyce's dinner into containers to take upstairs. This was going to take some planning, they could tell. Everything they did had to be done as a pair. One of them would always have to be on the lookout for house parents. They weren't worried about the other kids. The kids didn't usually ask too many questions.

They got the food upstairs. Joyce ate hungrily. She told Stacey and Angel that her family didn't eat that well. "Never enough money for food. Always enough for beer though." After eating, they put the dishes in a bag they had taken from the kitchen. They would take it back down when they had to go for study hall.

After study hall Stacey and Angel rushed back to their room. All was well. Joyce was asleep in the bed. They guessed that it had been a while since Joyce had had a really good night's rest. The girls got themselves ready for bed and joined Joyce. They all got a good night's sleep. The events of the day had worn them all out.

After breakfast the next morning, Angel asked Mrs. Barty if she could have a friend over for a few hours after school. They just wanted to hang out in her room for a while. Mrs. Barty said that would be fine. "This will work good, Angel told Stacey, we'll be pretty well covered for another night." While Mr. & Mrs. Barty were in the office, readying everyone for school, Joyce was able to slip out of the building. She would meet the girls a little ways down Seminary Ave. and they would all walk to school together.

Joyce came home with the girls after school. Mrs. Barty welcomed her. The girls had a fun evening visiting with the other girls in the dorm, experimenting with their hair and make-up. Joyce had dinner there, actually eating in the dining room this time. It was Friday night and the kids were allowed to stay up later, usually watching television.

At bedtime, Mrs. Barty asked, "Where's Joyce?"

Angel told her that her mom had picked her up. Angel said, "Joyce told me to thank you for the fun evening."

The beds were a little crowded that night. The first night was fun, the second not so much. Stacey told Angel, "We need a sleeping bag."

"Where are we going to get one, asked Angel?"

Stacey said, "You know, ask Andy Moss. He always seems to have access to everything around here. And he's always stashing things away."

Angel approached me on Saturday and asked if I knew if there was a sleeping bag around the home. "What for?" I asked. Angel reluctantly told me what was going on. I couldn't believe what they were doing, but understood. I knew Joyce. I did know where a sleeping bag was and would get it for her.

Every once in a while a house father got it in his head that a "camp out" would be fun. Some of the boys liked these and some didn't. There was a storage area on the main floor, between the office and the extra room that was used as a "sick room," where kids were sometimes required to stay if they had measles, mumps, a bad cold or something that could be passed around. I had remembered helping the last house father put a couple of sleeping bags on the top shelf of that storage area. I hoped no one would ever find them. I was one of the boys that didn't care for camping. I retrieved one of the bags, gave it to Angel and said, "Good luck."

Joyce used the bag for the next few nights. It wasn't ideal, but it worked. She didn't have pajamas with her and slept in her clothes, even wore her jewelry to bed. Not that she had a lot of jewelry, but she did have a cheap "friendship" ring she wore that someone had given her.

Saturday was a little more troublesome hiding out Joyce. Kids were coming and going. Chores had to be done. House parents were all over the building. The girls on the dorm were getting suspicious of Angel and Stacey's door being closed all the time. And someone had remarked at dinner on Saturday evening that Angel's appetite seemed to be getting bigger. Angel sure hoped that I could keep a secret.

Sunday was easier. Angel and Stacey had to attend church, so Joyce had the room to herself. Sunday dinner was served at the main building and a rest hour was required in the afternoon. Church again on Sunday evening. These were times that they didn't have to worry about "hiding" Joyce. They were once again able to get some extra food from dinner for her.

On Monday morning, Joyce slipped out of the dorm early. She told the girls, "I will meet you at school, at our usual spot." Actually, Angel and Stacey were kind of glad that she left early. They really liked and cared about Joyce, but this was getting kind of difficult. It had sounded like a lot more fun when they first talked about it.

When Stacey and Angel got to school, they immediately went to the bathroom where the three girls always met, but Joyce was not there. One of her other friends, Nancy Milar, said to Angel, "Joyce is gone. She left this note." Angel read the note.

Dear Stacey & Angel,

Thank you for your help these past few days. It was a blast, but I know I can't stay at the home for long. It is too difficult for the two of you. I don't want to get you into trouble. I am going to run away. Not sure where I will end up,

but I have some ideas. I will let you know when I get there.
Thanks again!

Love you both,
Joyce

Angel and Stacey felt terrible and were really worried for Joyce. They knew Joyce was tough and knew how to take care of herself. They figured they would eventually find out where she had gone. They hoped she would be safe.

No one from the home ever found out that Joyce had been "stowed away" at the home for those four days and nights. Only Angel, Stacey and I knew. It would always be our secret.

That evening, Angel returned the sleeping bag to me. She thanked me for my help and asked that I "never tell a soul." I assured her that her secret was safe with me.

I took the bag to put it back in storage. As I was lifting the bag, something dropped on the floor. It was Joyce's friendship ring. It must have come off in her sleep. I wondered if I should return the ring to Angel or Stacey. I said to himself, "Nah, no one will know it's missing and we'll probably never see Joyce again. If it ever should come up, I can always return it."

The ring went into my strongbox. It always brought back kind of a bittersweet memory. I was proud of Angel and Stacey for the way they had gone to bat for their friend. It also helped me to remember that even though the kids from the home thought they had it "tough," there were always other kids out there that had it even worse.

Chapter 25

THE BULLY

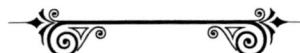

O uch! That must have really hurt. Why did Ernest slug Brad? He hit him right on the jaw. Brad's lip is swollen and I'll bet his jaw is going to bruise. It will turn all kinds of colors—purple, yellow and green. Brad staggered back against the kitchen counter after being struck by Ernest, but he didn't fall. He didn't cry either. Why didn't he fight back? It seems that whenever Ernest attacks anyone, they never fight back.

My powers of detection are evading me on this one. Why does Ernest insist on punching other boys? Sometimes he not only punches, but kicks and knees people. He seems to be so angry. I get angry and I know that other boys get upset, but they don't bully people. Sure, there are occasional fist fights, shoving matches and boys rolling around on the floor wrestling, but Ernest is always just flying off the handle. Many times there doesn't seem to be any reason for the outburst.

There was always a bully at the home. They came and went just like anyone else. They all resembled each other. They were usually bigger and stronger than most of the other boys and all seemed to have anger issues. It appeared that one bully would leave and the home would "special order" another.

Being a good detective, I referred to "Mr. Webster." The dictionary defines a bully as, "a person who hurts, frightens, or tyrannizes over those who are weaker or smaller." I guess that means that a bully bullies simply because he can. There has to be more to it than that. I am going to observe Ernest (from afar, of course) and try to reconcile in my mind what drives or possesses him.

When Ernest slugged Brad, Brad was just talking to one of the girls from the home that Ernest liked. Brad was not flirting with or touching her. They were having a conversation about school. Ernest just walked up to him, didn't say a word, and slugged him. Martha was aghast and let Ernest know. Ernest didn't even apologize. He just sauntered away and went to his room.

I did a little investigating by asking some of the other boys if they knew what had happened. It was the next day and everyone seemed to have their own version of the story. One of the boys, Marvin, had a little background. I guess that Ernest had just gotten into trouble in his last class of the day. He was apparently looking for someone to take his anger out on and Brad just happened to be there.

A few days later several of us students were in the lunch line at school. I was standing a few feet behind Ernest. In front of Ernest was a small boy, Ken. It didn't appear that there was any dialogue between them. The line was moving slowly and I could see that Ernest was getting antsy. All of a sudden Ernest grabbed Ken by the shoulders and pushed him to the concrete floor of the lunchroom, and hollered, "Why don't you get moving? I'm hungry!" Several students went to Ken's aid and helped him up. Someone further back in line let Ken "butt in." Probably because other students were scared, no one reported the incident and the lunchroom attendant had not noticed the commotion.

Again, I tried to find out what had caused Ernest's outburst. I was told that he had made a pass at a girl earlier that morning and had been rebuffed. Really? Like this hasn't happened to all of us? Someone needed to get Ernest some counseling. He was really going to hurt someone at some point.

Nathan arrived at the home on a gray, drizzly afternoon in November, just before the other kids were arriving from school. The house parents, Mr. & Mrs. Meyer, gave him a tour of the Harrison House and showed him his room. They told him his roommate would be a boy named Ernest. Ernest was a year older than Nathan. Mr. Meyer wondered if he should warn Nathan about Ernest's temper, but decided against it. He didn't want to provide fodder for a relationship that could turn sour from the beginning.

Nathan sat in the office when the other kids came home. Nathan thought to himself, "How am I supposed to remember all of these names?" He felt shy and embarrassed, but then realized that each one of these kids had gone through this same process at some point. So he decided to just "buck up" and live with it.

It was my turn to meet Nathan. Mrs. Meyer said, "Nathan, this is Andy Moss. He is our 'resident detective' here at the home." Nathan grinned, with a little puzzled look, and shook my hand. I instantly liked him. Mrs. Meyer told me that Nathan would be rooming with Ernest. I could feel the hairs standing up on the back of my neck. Nathan seemed like a nice kid. I hoped that Ernest was not going to bully him too.

At that moment Ernest arrived. He looked sullen. "Oh boy," I thought, "what set him off now?"

Mrs. Meyer turned to Ernest and said, "Welcome home, Ernest. I would like to introduce you to your new roommate, Nathan. Nathan just arrived. Please make him feel welcome."

Nathan extended his hand and remarked, "Do they call you Ernie?"

Ernest turned red and shot back, "Nobody but my dad calls me Ernie. Got it?" Nathan withdrew his hand and sat back down. Ernest stormed off.

I said, "Oh, Oh," under my breath. I was going to have to nip this situation in the bud. Things were already looking precarious.

It didn't take long for me to find the root of Ernest's recent outrage. One of the other boys told me there was going to be a fight at school tomorrow between Ernest and a local boy. The other boy's name was "Buck." He was a greaser. He always wore jeans with the bottoms rolled, no belt, shirts that were too tight and with an extra button open at the chest. He also wore a thick, silver chain around his neck that I guess he thought made him look tough. Buck and his greasy friends liked to hang out on a corner of the square, right where Main Street enters the square, and intimidate people. In those days, Bowman Shoes was on one corner and Wien's was on the other.

Apparently, someone had broached the subject of whc was "tougher," Ernest or Buck. Both boys were known around school as "hard guys." A boy named Cliff had suggested that the issue be settled. Buck and Ernest both agreed Neither one could turn the suggestion down and look like he was a "chicken." So the stage was set. After the two boys had lunch tomorrow, they would have a fight on the tennis court, located behind Clarence Olson Junior High and settle the issue once and for all.

Being the nosy detective that I was, I just couldn't quit worrying about Nathan. I ran into him in the bathroom. I said, "This is probably none of my business, but I like you and want to make you aware of something."

Nathan looked a bit confused, but said, "Let's hear it."

I told him about Ernest's reputation as a bully and also told him about the upcoming fight. I told him that was probably the reason why Ernest was so rude today. I warned Nathan, "Just try to stay out of his way tonight." Nathan thanked me for the warning and went to his room.

From the moment I arrived at school the next morning, I noticed the student body was abuzz with the pending confrontation. Everyone seemed to know about it and a lot of kids had their opinion about who the winner would be. I passed Buck in the hall that morning. He had that usual smirk on his face. When I saw Ernest in the hall he looked serious. Not only did he want to be the toughest guy in school, but he also wanted to show that the kids from the home were not going to be pushed around.

The bell rang, signaling the end of fourth hour and time for lunch. Students hurried to their lockers to unload books, gather their lunches and head to the "multi-purpose" room, as the lunch room was called. The room was used for dances, parties, meetings and other activities. The tables pulled down from the walls for eating.

All eyes were on the two boys during lunch. Ernest sat with a couple of his friends from town. Buck was at the other end of the room, sitting with a group of his friends. Both boys finished eating at about the same time. They eyed each other and stood up. There was a collective gasp in the room. I don't think the two teachers supervising the room had heard about the fight. They had kind of a bewildered look on their faces when nearly everyone in the room began to exit at the same time.

Buck, being closer to the exit, went out first, smirking and swaying his hips, trying to look cool and tough at the same time. Ernest and his buddies followed a few steps behind. Nearly the entire student body followed them out to the tennis court area.

The boys faced off. Buck, still smirking, had his hands in his pockets, feet spread wide apart. He taunted Ernest, "You go first, tough guy." With that, Ernest straightened his body, planted his feet firmly, reared back, and solidly slugged Buck right in the mouth. A combination of blood and chocolate from something he had for lunch, gushed from Buck's mouth. Before Buck could respond, Ernest punched him in the gut. Buck doubled over, then sat down on the ground and said, "You win, I give up." Turns out Buck wasn't much of a fighter; he was all talk.

The crowd roared its approval. You would have thought this was a fight at Madison Square Garden. I wonder if any bets were placed. Buck and his friends remained where they were, looking dejected and defeated. Ernest simply walked away. I was proud of him. A kid from the home was now offi-cially, the "toughest guy in school." As he walked back to the school, kids cheered him on. He just walked with his head held high. I wondered to myself if this was a good thing or bad thing in the life of Ernest Walker. Would this make him more of a bully or it would it establish in his mind that he had once and for all proven himself?

The following Saturday, Ernest had mowed a lawn on West Judd Street and was walking home. He was on the sidewalk running along the S & H Green Stamp Store, located at the corner of West Judd and Throop. He heard a voice from behind and turned around. There were three guys. He recognized Jon Nielsen. Jon's family lived around the corner. Jon had a reputation of being really tough and he was friends with Buck. Ernest had seen the other guys around town, but didn't know their names. The three quickly surrounded Ernest and pushed him up against the store wall.

Jon slapped Ernest with a backhand. Ernest was going to respond, but the other two guys grabbed him and held him back. Jon hit him in the stomach, knocking the wind out of him, and then threatened, "If I ever hear about you beating up one of my friends again, we will look you up and give you a beating you will never forget." Then the three guys just walked away.

Ernest was not aware that I had seen what happened. I, too, had been working in the neighborhood, and had stopped at Home Oil Company to get a pop from their vending machine. Although I saw the whole incident, I never mentioned it to Ernest. I didn't want to embarrass him and was also afraid he might take his frustration out on me.

The fight with Buck was the last I saw of Ernest's fighting. I think he learned a lesson from the incident with Jon Nielsen. I think he learned that no matter how big you are or how tough you think you are, there is always someone tougher. I am sure he was thankful that no one had seen the incident (except me, which he was not aware of). I'm sure he didn't want to be mocked like Buck had been.

I do know that the home heard about the altercation with Buck. Ernest was required to spend extra time with the home's social worker at the time, Mr. Hartley. Apparently, Mr. Hartley was able to delve into Ernest's past and help him to understand why he had such anger issues.

Not too long after Ernest's fight with Buck, he left the home. We were told that he was being taken to live with an aunt and uncle who lived in North Dakota, far away from Ernest's parents, who lived in Harvard, Illinois. The aunt and uncle were good Free Methodists and were planning to have

Buck attend high school at Wessington Academy, which was also run by the Free Methodist Church.

Shortly after Ernest's departure, a meeting was held with the home's director, the social worker and the house parents for the teenagers. The home had become a little disconcerted about Ernest's attitude and wanted the teens to understand why he acted like he did. They also wanted the kids to know how to better deal with bullying situations in the future.

We were told that Ernest had come from a very abusive home. The father had a bad temper, which he lost easily and frequently. He had on numerous occasions hit Ernest's mother and was constantly verbally abusive to her. Ernest received the same kind of treatment. He was spanked with whatever tool was handy at the time—a belt, a willow switch or a board. As Ernest got older, the father took to slapping, shoving and hitting with his fists. The immediate reason that Ernest had been brought to the home was that his father was once again striking Ernest's mother, and Ernest had tried to intervene. The situation got out of hand and the police were called. For his protection, Ernest was removed from the family home.

Mr. Hartley explained to us that many times bullies are created by their environment. As a result, it is the only way they know how to express their own hostilities. And in cases like Ernest's, the boys are frustrated because they are not yet big enough to deal with the abuser. That is why they generally pick on smaller kids–it is what they have learned. This type of person has a lot of pent up anger that needs to be released. They need to be taught to release it in a more positive manner, such as through physical labor or playing sports. Mr. Hartley explained that many times these children do not receive the proper training and/or counseling and this type of behavior just recycles itself.

Rev. Redding, the Executive Director of the home, told us that we need to report any incidences of bullying. Not only did the home not want any children to be hurt, but they also wanted to be able to provide proper support for the abuser.

About a month after Ernest left the home, a friend of mine from school, Bob Johnston, said he had something he wanted to give me. It was a thick silver chain. Bob told me that it was Buck's neck chain. It had fallen off in the fight. Bob had picked it up but was not sure what he should do with it. He didn't want to give it back to Buck, so he just put it in his locker and kind of forgot about it. He noticed it one day and thought perhaps I would like to have it since Ernest had lived at the home.

Bob was correct. I was glad to get the chain. I took it home and hid it in my strongbox. I sure didn't want Buck to ever find out that I had it. Every time I see the chain I wonder about Ernest. I feel badly about the issues in his life that were not of his own making. I hope his life got better. It also made my think about bullying and how I should attempt to prevent any such acts in the future.

Chapter 26

MY BEST FRIEND

I have never had a lot of close friends. Most people I know have one or two very close friends that they have had for years. They share intimate secrets. They help each other work through personal problems. They have fun together. Most of my friends are more of an "acquaintance." So many kids go through the home that you just don't get a chance to develop deep friendships. And it seemed that every time I tried to have a close relationship with someone from school, some rule at the home would preclude me from attending some activity and the friendship would just peter out. Additionally, I have always spent so much time working that I didn't have a lot of time to spend on relationships.

There was one boy associated with the home that I did become "best friends" with. His name was Jerol DeVore.

Jerol's parents worked at Sunset Manor, the senior home across the street that was also run by the Free Methodist Church. Jerol's dad was a former minister. He and his wife ran the kitchen and performed some other duties for Sunset Manor. They lived in an apartment located adjacent to the rest home. They had moved here from Kansas.

Jerol had an older sister, Mary. She was a very pretty girl. She was in high school. He had an older brother, Vic. Vic had a really cool older car. It was a convertible from the 1940's, but I can't remember exactly what make or year. Jerol also had another older sister, Rosalie. She was married to Marvin Gearhart. They moved to Woodstock along with Jerol's family and became house parents at the main building, for the boys there. Mr. Gearhart was one of my favorite house parents. He liked sports, just like me and Jerol. He was a good role model.

I was in sixth grade when Jerol and I met. He was a year older. We hit it off immediately. We were both very interested in sports. We naturally both liked girls. We attended Olson Junior High together. We walked to school together in the morning and walked home together in the afternoon. We would "shoot baskets" nearly every afternoon at his residence, where he had a backboard and net hung on a tree. I always enjoyed that activity, even though Jerol would generally beat me at playing "horse."

Jerol's family was a good influence for me. They were a good Christian family and would include me in a lot of their activities. I remember I had my first pizza at their place. I recall that I was going to eat it with a fork! It was nice that I had someone to associate with that had to live by basically the same rules as I did. At the same time I was allowed to share in their family setting—something I really craved.

Jerol and I never got into any trouble. We were just two young guys that loved sports and had a lot in common. We looked out for each other and shared experiences. It was not always the most convenient thing having his sister as a house parent, but it didn't really cause problems. Some of the other boys felt that I got some special privileges because my best friend was related to the house parents. Maybe I did.

I do remember one sad incident. Jerol got into a fight with one of the guys from school. Oddly, that young man had lived at the children's home for a couple of years during elementary school. Jerol was new to the school and all the kids, except for me, were cheering for the other guy. I don't remember how the fight turned out, but I really felt bad for my best friend. All other memories of my time having Jerol as my best friend are so positive.

Jerol's family did not live in Woodstock very long. I think they left after a couple of years. I know Jerol and I were not in high school together. They moved back to Kansas. I'm sure Jerol and I probably wrote each other a few times and Mr. & Mrs. Gearhart shared some information about him, but the distance was just too great to maintain a friendship and we lost contact.

I know that Jerol played high school sports and did well. I was told that he went on to Witchita State University. At some point I had seen a picture of him running for the track team. That is the last thing I ever heard of Jerol.

I am sure that Jerol had a successful life. He was that kind of person. Hard working, loyal and smart. I have tried in recent years to locate him, but have had no success. I would like nothing better than to track him down (I guess I need to put Andy Moss's detective skills to work) and at least have a conversation with him. I would love to know of his work, family and life.

Sadly, I have nothing from my time with Jerol to put in my strongbox. Only memories.

ABOUT THE AUTHOR

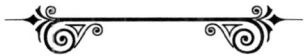

The author, Bill Anderson, lived in the Woodstock Children's Home for 11 years. He lived in the town of Woodstock, Illinois, until the age of 50. He served on the city council for eight years and served four years as Mayor of Woodstock. He wrote an autobiographical memoir of his 11 years at the home entitled, The New Kid, under the pen name of Andrew Moss, published in 2014. Anderson and his wife Deborah are now retired and reside in Oklahoma.

CPSIA information can be obtained at www.ICGtesting.com
Printed in the USA
LVOW10s2210161215

466865LV00023B/714/P